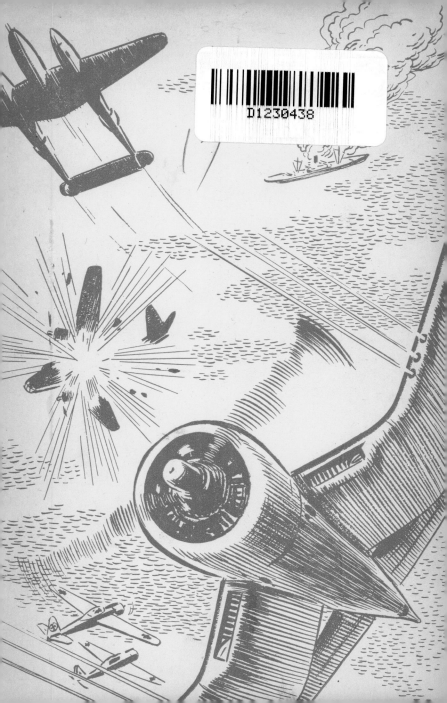

RED RANDALL ON NEW GUINEA

RED GAPED WIDE-EYED AT THE JAP AIRFIELD.
"QUITE A PRIZE, EH?" MAJOR WILKINS MURMURED.

Red Randall on New Guinea

Red Randall

ON NEW GUINEA

By

R. Sidney Bowen

 This book, while produced under wartime conditions, in full compliance with government regulations for the conservation of paper and other essential materials, is **COMPLETE AND UNABRIDGED**

GROSSET & DUNLAP

PUBLISHERS   NEW YORK

CONTENTS

RED RANDALL ON NEW GUINEA

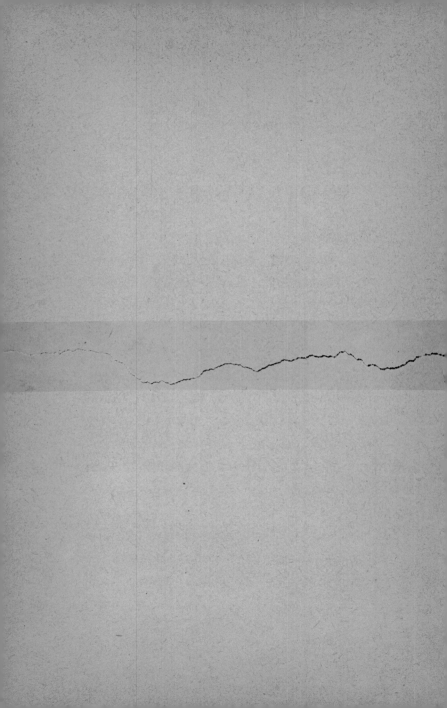

Chapter I

WAR BIRDS GATHER

SHE HAD once been a man-made bird of gleaming beauty that rode the skies from Glendale Airport, Los Angeles, to La Guardia Field, New York. From her rounded nose to her tail rudder she had been the last word in commercial air travel and the pride of the fleet. She had carried ambassadors, visiting potentates, movie stars, and all kinds of celebrities in her luxuriously appointed passenger cabin. She had held the record from Los Angeles to New York. She had been something to see in the air. She had been something to ride in.

But that had been long ago—before that December Sunday in Nineteen Forty-one when the savages of Nippon had screamed "Banzai!" and set forth to make the greatest mistake ever made by any nation in history. She was not a thing of beauty now. Her sides and wings were a dirty brown, and here and there patches covered holes made by Jap aerial machine-gun bullets. Her luxurious cabin fittings had been ripped out, and folding metal benches now were fitted along either side. Even her name, *Sky Queen*, was gone. Now she was just a DC-3, of the U. S. Army Air Forces. In short, she was a once-beautiful air liner taken over by the Government for air transport duty in war-torn skies.

At the moment she was drumming along up the eastern coast of Australia toward the base at Townsville. Aboard her were some much-needed medical supplies. But mostly her cargo consisted of humans—twenty-five fighter pilots who had been picked up from various other air bases located about the Continent of Down Under. These grim-faced young airmen were on their way to Townsville, and from there to . . .

But there were a lot of guesses about their final

destination. One, though, seemed more likely than the others. That was New Guinea. If Australia was to be saved New Guinea must be held at all costs. If New Guinea fell, New Caledonia would fall, and New Zealand, too. And then the land of the kangaroo would be completely encircled and helpless.

Yes, it was to be New Guinea. There seemed to be no doubt about that. Two of the fighter pilots aboard that transport were willing to bet their shirts on it. One was Captain Red Randall. The other was his flying pal and closest friend, Captain Jimmy Joyce. They did not rate themselves as military experts, but they had battled in the Southwest Pacific long enough to realize of what value New Guinea was to the enemy.

"Well, there's one thing, kiddo," Red Randall was saying to Jimmy, "and in my book it's something."

"It would be nice to know what you are raving about," Jimmy said. "Or were you clearing your throat just now?"

"I'm talking about New Guinea, what else?" Randall snorted. "All of us here are fighter pilots, so it means we're going to have a chance at single-seaters for a change. I'll like that, personally."

"I'll like it, too," Joyce said, and then stopped to look at Randall sharply. "Or would that be your idea of a crack because you and I have been in a two-seater quite a bit of late?"

"Oh, perish the thought!" Randall cried in mock horror. Then more seriously, "But I really didn't mean it as a crack, Jimmy. What I meant was that it will be nice to go up against the Nips with something just as good as they've got and maybe better."

"Yeah, at certain altitudes, of course," Jimmy replied. "High up, though, their Zero can do plenty against a Kittyhawk or an Airacobra."

"Depends on the pilot in the Yank ship," Randall said with an expressive wave of his hand. "When we get there I'll show you what I mean."

"Do that, by all means!" Joyce snapped. "I'll just love to watch you, you wonderful birdman!"

Red laughed. "Kidding aside, Jimmy, it will be something. Whether we go up after them, or make them come down."

"Well, so long as they come down, and not us, I'll be satisfied," Joyce murmured. "I agree with you; it will be good to go after them in a real airplane, and not some slow twin-engined job like this thing. It will be tough, though. A couple of days ago I was talking with a lad who had just come back from Seven Mile Field at Port Moresby. He said you meet a hundred Japs every time you go up. And when you come down to refuel, another hundred come over and bomb the daylights out of you. I gathered that none of the airfields around Port Moresby are what you would call health resorts."

Randall turned to peer out of one of the transport's windows. "Getting close to Townsville. I think I spot it up ahead. This is quite a country. I like it plenty. A fellow could do a lot worse than live in this part of the world."

"I'll tell the Chamber of Commerce president

when he comes in," Jimmy said. As the transport's twin Wrights were throttled and the big ship went slanting down by the nose, he added, "Pick yourself a cigar, friend. For once you hit the bull's-eye. It's Townsville ahead, all right."

Randall made sure, as did all the others aboard, that he had all of his gear with him. It amounted to little enough, but just the same he did not want to leave any of it behind. If you left something aboard a DC-3, the chances were you would never see it again. Forty-eight hours from now this transport might be in China, or on its way to the Middle East.

The transport circled the base at Townsville, received permission to land, and slid down to a graceful landing. It had been hot enough flying in the "tin goose" but when Randall and Joyce climbed down onto the ground, they felt as though they were walking through the door of a blast furnace. Young Joyce groaned and shielded his eyes against the terrific glare.

"What was that about a guy doing worse than sizzling in this place?" he demanded of Randall.

"Australia is a big country," Red retorted. "I didn't mean just here. Kind of warm, isn't it?"

"Warm!" Joyce exclaimed and cast disgusted eyes about the sun-baked field. "A guy would think you had Fiji Island blood in you. Oh, for a cake of ice! It would last for five seconds, anyway. Hey! Look at the ships, will you! Maybe they're for us, huh? But it will be calling it close to get one of those from here to New Guinea."

Randall glanced at the P-40's and P-39's dispersed about the field and shrugged.

"Maybe it isn't New Guinea," he said. "But if it is, we can carry wing tanks, you know."

An Air Forces major, wearing shorts and a sun helmet, approached the group with a flight board tucked under his arm. He grinned at them all as he pulled up to a halt.

"Welcome to the hottest spot this side of you-know-what, fellows," he said. "I'm Major Rankin, a sort of Johnny-on-the-spot around here. I've got some food and some cool stuff to drink, all waiting for you. But first, yell out as I call your names, will you?"

The Major took the flight board from under his arm and started calling out names from a list thumbtacked to it. There were twenty-five in all, and all twenty-five responded.

"Check," the Major said, tucking the flight board back under his arm. "Nobody missed the bus. Now, follow me, and I'll show you to the chow hall. After you've finished, the Colonel will be in to talk to you."

"About what, Major?" somebody asked.

Major Rankin grinned and poked a finger toward the north.

"About New Guinea, of course," he said. "That's where you boys are headed. Seven Mile Field at Port Moresby, to be exact. And I don't envy you. I've been there. Come along now. Everything is on the house here. At Seven Mile you'll have to scratch for what you get."

Chapter II

AN INTERRUPTED
LECTURE

COLONEL GORDON, Commanding Officer of the Army Air Forces base at Townsville was a frail-looking man, not a fraction over five feet six inches tall. He had a pair of steel-blue eyes, though, and a way of rippling his jaw muscles that made you forget all about his size. He made you think of a fighter. And that's just what he was. If you did not want to believe that he himself had earned the two rows of World War I and World War II ribbons under his wings, you could look him up in official records and become fully convinced.

He slipped into the chow room almost unnoticed. Not until Major Rankin spotted him and

called for attention did more than two or three
know that he was there. And he proved the kind
of officer he was by grinning and waving to them
all as he slipped into a chair at the end of the
long table.

"Go ahead and finish, fellows," he said in a
quiet but surprisingly clear voice. "What I've got
to say can wait a little while longer without chang-
ing the war one way or the other."

But there was no finishing up to be done. No
one was more interested in food than in what the
Colonel had to say. They all sat back in their
chairs and gave him their respectful attention. He
grinned and shrugged.

"Okay, if you want to hear it first," he said.
Then leaning forward on the edge of the table, he
started talking. "As you all probably know, you're
heading for Seven Mile Field at Port Moresby to do
any job up that way that Major Pratt, your C.O.,
will want you to do. The Japs want Port Moresby
bad, real bad. And they are going to throw the

book at us in an effort to take it. In case you are wondering, let me assure you that the Japs in New Guinea have *everything* to throw at us—bombers, fighters, troops, guns, *and* their navy!"

Colonel Gordon paused to lick his lips and swallow.

"And what we've got to throw back at them you could hide under your hat!" he said bluntly. "General MacArthur has some Australian and American troops on New Guinea. He has some light bombers and some fighters. But that's all. The Coral Sea and the waters about New Guinea are far too dangerous for American Navy ships right now. We haven't got the strength, yet, to go into those waters. So General MacArthur has to use something in place of the Navy. And that something will be pilots and airplanes. Almost everything that goes into New Guinea is flown in. We do have a couple of cargo ships, but it is anybody's guess how long it will be before Jap bombers will catch up with them. General Mac-

Arthur is relying almost one hundred per cent on aircraft to do the necessary jobs for his ground force."

The Colonel paused again as though to allow time for the seriousness of his words to sink in. There was no grin on his lips now. His face was grim and tight, and there was a meaningful glitter in his steely blue eyes.

"It's been one mighty tough job to hold Port Moresby from the very beginning," he went on speaking presently. "And it's going to be a whole lot tougher before we win. And we've got to win or clear out of this part of the world entirely. Let the Japs knock out our supply lines to Australia, and Australia will be through.

"It would be a much, much easier job to accomplish if General MacArthur had all the planes and pilots that he needed. But he hasn't got them. Just the same he is not going to wait for the Japs to come to him. He's going after the Japs with everything that he has. And heaven knows it's little enough."

Colonel Gordon stopped talking, but nobody moved. They were being told the facts. They weren't being kidded about a single thing. Colonel Gordon was the kind of commanding officer who let you have it straight.

"The Japs know the pickle we're in," he went on speaking. "And how they know it! At Seven Mile, or at any of the other fields you may be sent to, you won't have a minute's rest. They'll be after you when you're in the air, and they'll be after you when you're on the ground. They . . ."

At that instant the wail of the air-raid siren stopped the Colonel cold. He jumped to his feet.

"See what I mean?" he barked. "The rats will play in your front yard any time. Get out and pile into the slit trenches we've got here. I'll pick it up later."

The Colonel went out of the chow room door like a streak of lightning and tore over toward his office. The siren still wailed but the roar of engines, as the base's fighter protection ripped off the field, was just about drowning it out. Every-

body in the chow room shook himself loose and
went dashing outside. As one, they all peered
skyward, but momentarily the sun blinded them
and they saw nothing.

"They're up there, don't worry!" Major Rankin
shouted. "Come on. This way!"

No one lingered. They all lighted out after the
Major, selected a slit trench or foxhole, and piled
into it headfirst just as the field's anti-aircraft
guns opened up. By chance, Red Randall and
Jimmy Joyce picked on the same foxhole. They
tangled with each other as they went in, but came
up grinning wryly.

"No respect for age, have you!" Randall grunted
as he rubbed a bumped shoulder. "Such man-
ners."

An appropriate answer started off Joyce's lips,
when a stick of Jap bombs came down and struck
about two hundred yards from the field. The
roar that they made must have been heard clear
south to Melbourne. More Jap bombs piled down
but all of them missed the base by a good half

mile. Red and Jimmy could see the raiders now, eighteen of them in two groups of nine. They swung across the sky as though they were on strings. They were up about twenty thousand feet and the black puffs from the ack-ack guns were a good three thousand feet under them.

"Praise be, the Jap bombers are rotten shots!" Randall breathed as he raised an eye above the edge of the foxhole and looked at the P-40's and P-39's dispersed all about. "What a target for . . ."

And he stopped right there. A lone Jap bomb came down and practically plopped into the cockpit of a P-39. There was a puff of smoke, a mighty flash of flame, and then an earth-shaking roar. When the smoke blew away, the Airacobra had disappeared. There was nothing but a great yawning crater where it had stood. Luckily the planes on either side were dispersed far enough away so that flaming gas did not reach them.

"Did you mention something about rotten shots?" Jimmy Joyce shouted in his ear. "Maybe that was rotten aiming, but it was plenty lucky. I hope it wasn't the ship they were to give to me."

Randall cast his eyes aloft again, and saw something that gave him a sense of wild satisfaction. A P-40 had reached the altitude of the raiders. It practically shot the wings off a twin-engined Mitsubishi. The Jap plane staggered out of formation, then rolled over and dropped toward earth, leaving behind a long trail of flame and smoke.

"Nice!" Randall breathed. "That lad can shoot. And fly, too. Look at him cut for another one, Jimmy! Those Jap dopes! They always fly perfect formation like they were over Tokyo!"

It was true. Jap pilots in formation never seem to take evasive action against heavy flak or attack by fighter aircraft. When one is shot down, the next plane behind simply moves forward to fill the gap, and the whole formation wings steadily on its way like soldiers on parade. A costly way to raid, and it was proving to be so this time.

The Yanks were up there, now, and they were tearing in with all they had. Four Mitsubishis fell out of the first formation, and three toppled down from the second formation. But the remaining bombers doggedly kept on dropping their bombs, most of which missed the target completely. Eventually the Japs were past their target. Still in parade style, they wheeled out to sea and were soon lost in the distance.

"Seven out of eighteen, not a bad score for us," Randall grunted as he climbed out of the foxhole and brushed himself off.

"Not a bad score," Jimmy Joyce agreed, "but still less than a drop in the bucket. The rats most likely have seven hundred to replace the seven our boys got. Too bad the Colonel didn't order us to go up in the ships here. We could have wiped out the bunch of them."

"Exactly what I was thinking," Randall said, as they walked back toward the chow house. "He probably had his reasons, though."

That last was indeed true, and the Colonel spoke of it when they all were back at the long table again.

"You fighter pilots probably are wondering why I didn't order you to man those dispersed planes when the siren let go," he said with a half grin. "They are to be your planes, as a matter of fact. But those Kittyhawks and Airacobras are needed far more at Port Moresby than they are here. And as Jap bomb aiming is pretty sour, it was a better bet to leave them on the ground than to risk losing some of them in the air."

The Colonel paused and grinned broadly.

"Also, I want to keep peace in the family," he said. "My boys like to take care of the Japs themselves. And they did pretty well this time, as you all saw. They'd get peeved if outsiders went buzzing aloft to give them a hand. Now to get back to what I was talking about before we were interrupted."

The commanding officer glanced at the circle of faces, and went on:

assign you your planes. Try them out, but if we have any more raids, keep out of the way. Your ships are for Port Moresby. Besides, my boys wouldn't like it. They're a jealous bunch, bless 'em. Dismissed, and good luck to each and every one of you."

"There's just one thing I wish," Red Randall said several minutes later as Jimmy Joyce and he walked across the sun-flooded airfield.

"Such as what?" Jimmy asked.

"That we were going to serve under Colonel Gordon in New Guinea," Randall replied. "There's a commanding officer I could fly for in a big way."

"And that makes two of us," Jimmy Joyce agreed firmly.

Chapter III

HOT WELCOME

DAWN WAS just about one hour away, but the skies from east to west, and from north to south, were still solid black. In the Southwest Pacific, night falls suddenly and dawn arrives just as suddenly. There is no in-between period. Night swoops down to blanket everything, and dawn comes up in a rush of light.

On the American-made airfield at Cape York, the most northerly point in Australia, there was quite a bit of light, and a tremendous amount of activity. The light came from tiny flares set along the field's runway and from the exhaust plumes of Kittyhawks and Airacobras being revved up for flight. The activity was the ground crews and

22

pilots making sure that everything was set for the flight to Port Moresby.

Both Red Randall and Jimmy Joyce had been assigned a Kittyhawk, and each was fussing over his plane, preparing for the hop to New Guinea. They had test-flown their charges back at Townsville, made one or two adjustments, and flown with the others up to Cape York. During the trip north, a couple of other "bugs" became evident, which they now were eliminating. Other fighter pilots, too, were correcting minor flaws in their planes or engines. All this adjustment did not mean that the aircraft were old and unfit for active service. Every one of the P-40's and P-39's was in good condition. It was simply that every pilot likes certain things his way, and not as they are when the plane comes off the assembly line. It may be a different type of cushion in the seat, or the position of the throttle, or the way the aircraft is rigged, or any one of a thousand little things that are not important to anyone but him.

It was Red Randall who attained his personal

idea of plane "perfection" first. He legged down to the ground and walked over to Jimmy Joyce who was sitting in the cockpit of his P-40, fiddling with the safety harness.

"Aren't you set yet, kiddo?" he asked with a grin. "What are you trying to do with that safety harness? Fix it so you won't fall out in case you pass out from fright?"

"When a guy has to look out for himself, *and* somebody else, too, not to mention any names," Jimmy snapped, "he's a sucker not to make sure that his safety harness will hold. After all, I may have to kick her about plenty."

"Well, that's right nice of you, neighbor," Randall chuckled. "I'll remember that if a couple of the rats drop down on my tail."

"You'd better do a whole lot more than just remember," young Joyce said grimly, as he made a final adjustment of the harness and found it to his liking. "There might be two on my tail, and I wouldn't have time. Well, I guess she's all set now. There's Colonel Barber over there. It's time for that briefing he said he was going to give us. But I'd like to know why we need a briefing."

"Routine precaution, probably," Randall said as Joyce legged down. "Or maybe he just loves to talk to us. How would I know?"

"Did I ask you?" Jimmy said. "A lot of fuss, though, for a three hundred and fifty mile hop. I could make that with my eyes closed."

"Well don't, my friend," Randall said, as they walked over to where the others were grouping about the Cape York commandant. "We can't afford to lose even *one* plane!"

Young Joyce let that crack slide, and presently they had joined the group. Colonel Barber, a well-built, good-looking man in his late forties, counted noses, and when he saw that all were present began his briefing.

"Stick in a bunch from take-off until you get there," he said. "If one has to slow down, the others are to slow down with him. Come daylight there'll probably be quite a few Japs out on the prowl, and they like to pick on a lone tagging ship even more than the Nazis do. However, if one of you figures that he can't make it, signal the others and drop out and come back. Radio us the letters X,Y,Z, nothing else. We'll take a bearing on you from here, and come out looking for you in case you go down.

"Remember, now, get through if you can, but don't try to do it by stretching your luck. It will be much better to come back and get your plane fixed up than to try to bull your way through. We haven't nearly enough fighter planes and fighter pilots. We can't spare a single one of you. You are needed at Port Moresby bad. There are only twenty-five of you, but it's quite possible that you boys may be the difference between holding onto Port Moresby and being kicked out of New Guinea altogether. That's how tough the situation is there right at the moment."

The base commandant paused, stared for a moment at the grim, determined pilots standing before him, and went on speaking:

"You're all heading for Seven Mile Field, Major

Pratt in command. I know Major Pratt personally, and I can tell you that you'll find him one of the finest officers any of you have ever served under. He's already done wonders with the handful of pilots and planes we've been able to send him. And I know he'll do more wonders with you fellows. Pratt has been through the mill, so listen well to anything he may have to say to you.

"You all know the location of that strip of ground known as Seven Mile—at least you should from the study of the maps and air photos I gave you. Some of Pratt's pilots may buzz out and lead you in, *but* they may be busy with Jap raiders. In that case, don't attempt to land on Seven Mile. You'd better move on and land on Seventeen Mile Field, which is on the other side of the Goldie River."

"How about pitching in and helping out in the scrap, if there's one going on, sir?" somebody asked. "We're taking full ammo belts along with us."

The Colonel smiled faintly. "Your orders are to

get yourself and your plane to Major Pratt at Seven Mile," he said quietly. "But if a Zero should happen to drift across your sights, I wouldn't just blow kisses at the pilot if I were you!"

Everybody chuckled. The pilot who had spoken went beet-red and grinned sheepishly.

"I get it, sir," he said. "Off the record, eh?"

"Strictly unofficial," Colonel Barber said gravely. "I can only give you orders what to do. If Zeros necessitate a change of orders, then do what you think is best. Well, I guess that's all. Nice flying, and good hunting. Get into your planes, and get going, fellows. Fly the formation I plotted for you, keep it, get there, and give them the works."

With a nod and a grin the Colonel waved them toward their planes. Like schoolboys breaking class for recess, the fighter pilots spun around and raced toward their planes. A couple of minutes later the darkness that clung to Cape York vibrated and trembled with the roar of many reving engines. Soon the first three-plane element went ripping down the runway, cleared, and prop-clawed up into the air.

Red Randall led the second element off. Jimmy Joyce was on his right, and a pilot named Stacey was on his left. All three took off sweet as could be and climbed up to join the first element. The six planes started to circle the field and presently the others came up and dropped into position to form a huge V of V's with four planes making up the last element. Then the aerial armada straight-ened out on crow course for Seven Mile Field at Port Moresby and for whatever this new phase of the war against the monkey men of Nippon held in store for them.

Flying with the alert yet nonchalant ease that only comes to a pilot after considerable experi-ence, Red Randall slumped comfortably in his pit seat and let his thoughts wander. He had been much impressed by the talk Colonel Gordon had delivered back in Townsville. Had he been a green fledgling he would have regarded what the Colonel had to say as the old pep-and-fight line—a slight exaggeration of true facts so that the greenhorns would be sure to keep up on their toes.

But Randall was a veteran airman, and he knew that the Colonel had punched from the shoulder. It was truly bad on New Guinea. The Nips held all the good cards in the deck. But even so, General MacArthur was going to shove the few chips he had into the pot and play every card he had to the limit. It would take headwork, great courage, and the art of bluffing at the right time to hold out and win. But win they would, because win they *must!*

"And may I stand up under it and do my share!" Randall breathed softly to himself as his Kittyhawk drummed along. "I don't care what kind of a job I get to do, only that I'll be able to do it. Amen!"

Straightening up a bit in the seat, he glanced off to his right at Jimmy Joyce's plane. Dawn was really coming up now. A band of orange gold lined the eastern horizon and he could see Jimmy's helmeted head clearly. As though Jimmy had felt Red's eyes upon him, he turned his head and flashed a grin across the air space that separated the two planes. Randall grinned back, nodded, and held up two fingers in the V for victory sign.

During the few moments they had spent exchanging silent air greetings with each other, the dawn light had increased a hundred per cent. Down below Randall could see the endless swells of the pure blue Coral Sea. When he peered dead ahead, past the three-plane element in the lead, he thought he could make out the brownish black streak on the horizon that was the New Guinea coast line.

Sight of it started his heart hammering a little and a quiver of eager anticipation rippled through him. Somewhere ahead was to be "home" for awhile. How long, he had no idea. It might be that it would be his final home on earth, but he brushed that thought aside quickly. In war you thought a lot about death, but always about somebody else's death, not yours. You had a charmed life. You felt it inside. There was no bullet or bomb made yet with your name on it. If you did not feel that way, you went to pieces in no time and became a danger not only to yourself but to your comrades as well.

Another thought suddenly slipped into Randall's mind. He turned his head to the left and right, and twisted all the way around to count the planes. Including his own, they totaled twenty-five. No one had been forced to drop out and return to Cape York. No one had even had to cut down his speed and thus force the others to slow up. The Allison engines that powered the Kittyhawks and the Airacobras were living up to their reputations and not letting any pilots down. Everybody all present, flying right on schedule, and there was Port Moresby a few miles ahead.

And then, suddenly, four bunches of nine dots each appeared in the dawn-flooded sky ahead. Even as Randall caught sight of them, he saw tongues of flame and columns of sooty white

smoke belch up from the smudge line that marked
the coast of New Guinea.

A moment later Randall saw the first plane element start to pull away from him. He instantly
shoved his own throttle from cruising speed to
full out. His wing men, Joyce and Stacey, did the
same thing. So did everybody else in the formation. And twenty-five agate-eyed eagles went
thundering across the remaining miles of air toward the Jap bombers that were dropping death
and destruction on Port Moresby.

"Guess you had kind of a hunch, eh, Colonel
Barber?" Randall murmured, as he slid his thumb
up to the stick button that operated the electric
trigger mechanism of his guns. "Or maybe it
happens every time. Well, if they'll just stick
around long enough, I'm going to make certain
that a couple of them drift across my sights. And
it won't be kisses that I'll blow at the rats either!"

Chapter IV

WHERE IT RAINS NIPS

It took the formation of twenty-five fighter planes about four minutes to reach the coast of New Guinea. All the while Randall could see more bombs sending earth, flame, and smoke skyward. He saw Yank planes prop-claw up to give battle, and a great fear plagued him that the Nips would turn and run for safety before he could get a chance to use his guns.

But the Nips did not turn and run. Perhaps they did not see the twenty-five fighters thundering toward them. Perhaps they were so cocksure of themselves that they did not bother to look about the sky. Perhaps they were following the usual stupid Jap formula, that of flying crow-course to a point, dropping their bombs, and flying back like so many remotely controlled robots.

At any rate, the Japs came sailing across Port Moresby wave after wave. A couple of them turned into balls of fire and went tumbling down, but the others kept on going. Suddenly Randall spotted fifteen Jap Zeros. They hung in the air above the bombers, and Red wondered if they were going to wait until all the bombers were spilled before they piled down to take a hand.

It was strange to see those Zeros up there coasting about while their bombers were being winged. Like many times before, he was completely stumped by the workings of the Japanese mind. Regardless of what happened to change things, a Jap always followed a set battle plan. It seemed as though he had no sense of initiative. Cunning and tricky, right up at the head with the best, was the Jap—when he was winning. But once throw him offstride, and he was your pigeon for the taking.

And that was exactly what those twenty-five fighter pilots did to the Jap bombers. They went piling in with guns blazing and threw every Jap offstride. Being one of the first to reach the Jap formation, Red Randall soon got a Mitsubishi twin-engined job "drifting across his sights." He lined up the right outboard engine on the Jap plane and pressed his trigger button. The Kitty-hawk's guns sang their song of destruction. In the bat of an eye the Mitsubishi's right outboard engine caught fire, and the flame swept across the wing to envelope the rest of the aircraft. For some odd reason the burning plane flew a complete loop before it plummeted into the waters of Port Moresby harbor.

Randall did not take time out to watch it hit and explode. The instant the Mitsubishi's engine burst into flame he turned his attention elsewhere.

By this time the Zero pilots apparently had decided that they were fighting in the war, too. Down they came, their silverish wings flashing in the sun that was now well above the horizon, and each one was spraying four jetting streams of flame. Randall yanked his nose up toward one that was fairly near him and let drive. But he did not fire in time. He saw his tracers rip into the Zero's tail section, but the Jap plane simply swerved a little and kept right on rocketing down toward an Airacobra.

In a flash Red wheeled over on wing tip to rip down upon the Jap. But even as he did so, he caught sight of something out of the corner of his eye that made him forget the diving Zero. Offshore a way, two Jap Zeros were whirling like angry vultures about a B-26 Marauder light bomber. One glance told Randall that the B-26 was returning from a bombing raid of its own on perhaps Rabaul, or Buna, or Lae. At any rate it was in trouble. One of its engines had gone out, and the aircraft was struggling back to base on its other engine. Helpless to turn away from the air battle raging above, it was attempting to plod on through to its own field. Apparently the two Zeros had spotted it and had quit the fight high above to enjoy an easy kill of a cripple.

The sight filled Randall with cold rage. He

fed his roaring Allison every ounce of high octane it would take. His wings screamed in the wind as he sent the Kittyhawk ripping downward, and his air-speed indicator needle climbed all the way around the face of the dial. Hunched forward over the stick, eyes agate, and lips pressed tightly together to form a thin, grim line, Randall gave the Kittyhawk its head and fixed his eyes on the nearest Jap.

It seemed an eternity before he was able to lose sufficient altitude to get within gun range. The Zeros were riddling the crippled Marauder with their savage cross fire. The fact that only the tail turret gunner of the B-26 was returning the Zero fire indicated that there were wounded and perhaps dead men aboard. As Randall closed in, firing ceased spouting up from the tail turret guns—the lone gunner also had been put out of action.

Randall's bullets virtually shot the nearest Jap plane into a mess of smoking toothpicks. The light-constructed Zero took the full force of his fire and disintegrated into a shower of flaming embers.

Pulling up out of his dive slightly, Red cut his Kittyhawk off to the left and across the top of the Marauder to get at the Zero closing in from the other side. The Nip saw him coming, fired a quick short burst at almost point-blank range, and then took hasty evasive action.

Randall was on him in a flash. Almost nose to nose, his guns poured lead into the Nip. And that killer took it, practically straight in his face. His Zero streaked off for a short distance, and then seemed to hit an invisible brick wall suspended in mid-air. It folded up like a tired accordion, and fell down into the sea in flames.

"Two down, but good!" Randall muttered, and pulled up and around toward the crippled Marauder.

He gave a cry of alarm when he got a look at the bomber again. The Jap rats had struck home after all. The Marauder was on fire, and doomed. She was less than five hundred feet from the surface of the water and was losing altitude fast.

"Jump fellows, bail out!" Randall shouted impulsively.

He was now on a level with the B-26 and he could see the pilot half slumped over the controls. The man turned his face Randall's way. He seemed to smile a little, and raised one dangling hand in a gesture of farewell. The Marauder rolled over on one wing and seemed to hover between the sky and the water for a long moment before it dropped straight down by the nose and went flaming to its doom. It disappeared completely from view, leaving only a series of frothy white circles in the water that grew bigger and bigger until they had spent themselves and were gone.

Bitter anguish struck Randall. He smashed his clenched free fist against the side of his cockpit again and again. The repeated blows caused little needles of pain to dart up his arm, but he hardly felt them. To have arrived too late, to see brave men die helplessly, filled him with a hatred of the

Japs that would be with him the rest of his life.

"The skunks!" he rasped as he stared down at the circular ripples on the water. "The dirty killing skunks. I'll think of this moment always, every time I see one of them. So help me, I will!"

That vow made, Red hauled the Kittyhawk up for altitude, but then he realized that it was not a necessary maneuver. The air battle was over. The Mitsubishis and the Zeros still able to do so had turned tail and fled. The Yank planes were sliding down toward the airfields around Port Moresby. Near Port Moresby half a dozen columns of oily black smoke marked where Jap bombs had struck and scored on ammo dumps or fuel stores. Randall stared at them as he guided his Kittyhawk toward Seven Mile Field and wished with all his heart that he and the others had arrived just ten minutes sooner. They could have blocked off the Mitsubishis and either shot them down or sent them scurrying for safety.

"Too late, even if it wouldn't have been too

little," he murmured and sighed heavily. "Well, I know of three of the rats who'll never fly again. I wonder how many Jimmy got."

A few minutes later, when he slid down onto the bomb-pocked strip of earth that was Seven Mile Field, he was not interested in how many planes Jimmy had shot down. He was interested only in finding young Joyce. He did not see him among the tight-faced pilots that climbed out of their planes and walked slowly over to a little hut which served as the field's operations office. He bumped into young Stacey who had flown in his element, but Stacey could not help him out. He had lost track of Jimmy Joyce once the fight started, just as he had lost track of Randall.

"Others are still coming in," he said, pointing aloft. "Your pal is probably one of them. Anyway, I'm pretty sure he wasn't one of the three that the Japs caught."

"Three?" Red echoed and his heart seemed to skip a beat. "You mean three out of our flight from Cape York?"

"Three that I saw," Stacey replied gravely. "They sure weren't kidding us. This is really one hot corner of the war. We better get over to Operations, though. Major Pratt is probably there waiting for us."

Randall hesitated, glanced up at the five planes aloft, then dropped into step with Stacey. Right now the important thing was to report to Major Pratt, his new commanding officer. In the Operations Office, Major Pratt was seated at a table, checking off names on a list in front of him as each pilot came in. Red did not give his name immediately, for just then he spotted Jimmy Joyce, who had already reported in and was standing at the back of the room talking with some of the other pilots.

Their eyes met, and they grinned at each other. Red started to walk over to Joyce, but Major Pratt's long arm shot out and stopped him.

"Greetings later, Captain," he said in a firm quiet voice. "Your name, please?"

"Robert Randall, sir."

Major Pratt checked the name on the list, then looked up at him sharply and smiled.

"Heard of you, too, Randall," he said. "Very glad to have you with us."

"Thank you, sir." As Red looked into the calm blue eyes and at the rugged square jaw of Major Pratt, he knew at once that he was going to like his new C.O.

Then he moved over to where Jimmy Joyce stood waiting.

"Nice to see you, kiddo," he said in a low voice. "Had a little scare for a few minutes after I landed. Didn't see you about. You make out all right?"

"Worse than that!" Joyce said and made a face. "I only got one of them, and then my guns went haywire. Only sensible thing to do was sit down fast. I did, and watched the rest from the ground. From a foxhole, to be more specific. If we'd only reached here ten minutes sooner! How about you?"

"Three, but two of them got a Marauder I was

trying to save," Randall told him. "Plain slaughter. She was crippled. Only one engine. It was nasty to see, the rotten killers!"

Jimmy nodded, and started to speak, but stopped himself as Major Pratt rapped on the table for attention.

"Welcome to Seven Mile and New Guinea, gentlemen," he said. "I guess you all have a pretty good idea what it's like here. I want to thank you for arriving when you did and pitching in. The little show just over cost us four aircraft—a Marauder that went in offshore, as it was coming back from Rabaul, and three of your pilots. The count so far on the enemy is twelve bombers and seven Zeros. That's good, but you've got to make it even better next time. They have fifty planes to every one of ours, so you can see what I mean. We can lick them, though. And you'll help us prove that little item.

"Lieutenant Wilson, here, will show you where to bunk, and show you the ropes. Don't go straying off, though. Everybody at Seven Mile—

ground officers, pilots, and ground crewmen—is on twenty-four-hour duty. Be ready to hop into your ships and go Jap hunting at any time. I'll talk more with you later. Thanks for coming over. Believe me, it's good for all of us here to see you. Take over, Wilson, please."

The Major nodded to a sun-bronzed officer standing by the table, then picked up his papers and walked away. Lieutenant Wilson smiled at the newcomers and motioned them to follow him. Red Randall and Jimmy Joyce trailed along with the others.

"So this is New Guinea," Red thought. "New Guinea where it rains Nips. Three of the boys never even had a chance to touch their wheels to the surface of Seven Mile. They died in the air at the start. How many of the twenty-two left will meet the same fate in this corner of the war where the odds are fifty to one against you?" He shot side glances at the others walking along with him, and wondered.

Chapter V

A WEB OF MYSTERY

FOUR DAYS had passed since Red Randall and Jimmy Joyce had arrived at Seven Mile Field in the thick of a Jap air attack. For four days they had been constantly on the alert, but no Japs had returned for a repeat engagement. It was almost as though they had packed up and gone back to Tokyo.

Evidently the enemy had been caught off base that first day, and was now licking his wounds. Then, too, perhaps the weather had something to do with it. There was a lot of rain, and quite often fog completely hid the thirteen-thousand-foot peaks of the Owen Stanley Mountains which formed a natural barrier between the Jap forces at Buna and the Yanks at Port Moresby. It was a well-known fact that the Japs at Buna were chopping their way along the Kokoda Trail in an attempt to worm up and over the Owen Stanley range and descend upon the American and Australian troops. For that reason several reconnaissance patrols were flown over the treacherous range to spot Jap units and photograph them for Intelligence. Such patrols were not joyhops, and two pilots had failed to return. But as far as air action was concerned, there was none. The pilots went out on scouting patrols but they met not even a lone Jap.

"Japs twenty-four hours a day, they told us," Jimmy Joyce grunted as he and Randall were taking it easy in the shade of some oleander trees just off the landing strip. "Well, maybe so, but it sure doesn't seem like that."

Randall yawned. "The answer to that one is easy. They know you and I are here, fellow, and they're no dopes. They hole up, and stay that way."

"How the guy hates himself!" Jimmy laughed.

"Seriously speaking, I wonder what the answer really is. I've been talking with some of the old-timers around here, and they don't get it, either. They say this is the first lull since the Japs set up shop on this island. This waiting for something to happen makes me nervous."

"No rest cure at all," Randall agreed, and squinted at the Owen Stanley Mountains towering upward to the north. "I keep catching myself looking at those mountains and wondering if they are full of throat-cutting Japs just waiting for the word to come piling down on us. It wouldn't be nice if that happened, I can tell you."

"You don't have to!" Jimmy said with emphasis. "I can imagine that well enough myself. This whole doggone island gives me the creeps. One thing I hope is that I don't get forced down any place. Why, you could go down no more than a couple of miles from this very spot, and it would take you weeks to work your way back through the jungle. No, sir! I don't like this neck of the woods at all."

"And you've got a lot of company there," Randall grinned. "I understand that the Portuguese discovered New Guinea about the time the Pilgrims were going ashore at Plymouth Rock. Well, for my money the Portuguese can take it back and keep it, once we've thrown the Japs out. And . . ."

Randall cut the rest off short as at that instant the raid siren wailed. Instantly Red and Jimmy sprang to their feet and cast eyes skyward. They saw nothing but an empty vastness of blue and the ball of gold that was the sun. One fleeting glance upward and then they sprinted toward Operations to get orders for the approaching raid.

When they reached there, however, it was to learn that no Jap raid was in the offing. The siren had been blown merely to assemble all pilots. Major Pratt stood waiting in shorts and sun helmet. In his right hand he held some papers. As the pilots gathered about him, he folded the papers and stuck them in his pocket.

"No Japs on the way, so relax!" he called out and grinned. "That is, not on the way yet. But they will be soon, and in plenty of force, unless Intelligence got the picture all wrong. At ease, boys."

The pilots made themselves comfortable.

"For the last couple of weeks," the Major went on, "the Japs have been filling Rabaul Harbor with their supply ships. We know that the ships have come down from Truk in the Carolines. And I might add that it's broken our hearts not to be in a position to do something about it. We just haven't got the bombers. And the Zero umbrella the Japs keep over Rabaul all the time is much too tough for us to tackle with the few long-range fighter aircraft we've got. And so, all that we have been able to do is to keep our eyes on the Jap, check his movements as much as we could, and try to figure out what his next move will be. Is he planning to reinforce at Buna, or Gona, or any other of his positions on New Guinea? Has he been building up his supplies at Rabaul for a move southward to the New Hebrides or New Caledonia?"

The Major paused and studied the sea of faces for a moment.

"Intelligence thinks it has worked out the answer," he continued. "The Jap is heading for Port Moresby by way of Milne Bay. He has troops at Milne Bay now, but a much larger force is being moved over from New Britain. The Japs have been doing this at night, but Intelligence hasn't been asleep, so we know what they're up to. The drive up from Milne Bay may be planned to coincide with a Jap drive across the Owen Stanley Mountains. We don't know, but it's certainly a possibility. The Jap knows that as long as we continue to hold Port Moresby he can't hope for a successful attack on Australia. He knows that we'd cut his supply lines to ribbons. So Port Moresby must be his, and he's coming after it with everything he has. And you can bet your shirts that it will be plenty!"

The C.O. paused again as though to allow time for the meaning of his words to sink in.

"When he intends to pull the trigger on this

thing, we don't know," he presently went on speaking. "But you can bet that it will be soon. Our patrols working their way down Milne Bay way have run into some pretty tough opposition, which must mean that the Jap has just about assembled sufficient strength to get started. Anyway, we are going to try to beat him to the punch with what we have. Beginning today, all the bombers we have here at Seven Mile, as well as those at Seventeen Mile, Three Mile, Four Mile, and Twelve Mile Fields, are going to start plastering the Milne Bay area every hour on the hour. The job for all fighter pilots will be to keep the Zeros off the bombers, and to ground strafe every time they get the chance. If you see Jap boats offshore, go after them. In short, give them the old one-two punch continually. But not at the expense of our bombers, of course; they are your main responsibility.

"It's going to be tough, tougher than most of you probably realize. It stands to reason that once we start punching at Milne Bay, the Jap is going to move a good part of his Rabaul fighter umbrella over there. You'll be outnumbered ten to one, at least. Some of us are going to die in the next couple of days. We might just as well face that fact. But while we can, let's give those dirty rats everything we've got, and go down scrapping. We haven't any Navy to do this job, so we've got to act as the Navy and punch the daylights out of them in Milne Bay. If we do that the Jap drive will be delayed. And that is exactly what we want —time. Time so that troops, guns, and planes can be sent up here from Australia. They'll arrive eventually, plenty of them. But not tomorrow, or even next week. So it's up to us, and our troops here on New Guinea, too, to upset the Nip and hold him off just as long as we possibly can.

"Lieutenant Wilson has worked out the flight schedules. The first of the bombers go off at two o'clock this afternoon. I'll lead the first fighter escort, of course. That's all, and the best of luck to you. Take over, Wilson."

Ten minutes later Jimmy and Red had learned

that they were to fly escort for the second wave of bombers. They decided to check their planes once again to make sure that everything was in working order.

"Four hours more and then we take off!" Red said as he glanced at his watch. "I'm sort of glad, though, that we've really got a definite assignment. Those scouting patrols were beginning to get my nanny."

"Didn't care much for them myself," Jimmy murmured and squinted up at the sky. "But I guess this is really going to be something. The Major certainly doesn't pull his punches, does he?"

"Thinking about that 'some of us are going to die' remark?" Red asked and looked at him.

Young Joyce nodded. "It was in my mind," he admitted. "I would have been just as pleased if he'd skipped it. Of course, it's true. Gives you a funny feeling, though."

Randall silently searched Joyce's face.

"Such as, Jimmy?" he presently asked quietly.

"Not getting any dizzy hunches in that head of yours, are you?"

"No more than you have!" Jimmy said a trifle sharply. "Don't worry, though, the Jap rat hasn't been born, if you get what I mean."

"I do, and I feel better," Randall said with a grin. "It's not like you to have crazy ideas, Jimmy. You had me worried there for a minute. Well, we know now the answer to why the Japs haven't been doing much flying these last four days. Saving up for the big show, I guess."

"It's a good guess," Jimmy nodded.

At that instant they both heard the roar of a plane coming in toward Seven Mile fast and low. It was coming from the east but when they faced that way, they did not spot it for a few seconds. The plane was low, really low, and when they did sight it they both held their breaths in fear that the pilot would fly right into the tops of the jungle trees. It was a Yank plane, a Kittyhawk, and although its Allison engine sounded as though hitting on all cylinders, the aircraft was trailing a thin ribbon of dirty gray smoke.

"Who is he, and what's eating him, I wonder," Randall murmured, as the plane streaked down toward the landing strip. "The way he's coming in you'd think the whole Jap air force was on his tail."

"Sure looks in a hurry to get here," Jimmy agreed. "If he doesn't look out, he's going to overshoot."

"He *is* going to overshoot!" Randall cried out in alarm. "And he hasn't got his wheels down. What's the matter with the guy? Why doesn't he pull up and go around again?"

The Kittyhawk rocketed down like a runaway comet in high gear. As the plane streaked over them, Red and Jimmy spotted a couple of ragged patches on the near wing. The plane looked as though it had flown through heavy flak and wild tropical storms.

"He's going to crash!" young Joyce shouted and

started running. "He's going to crash! He's crazy to try it. What's wrong with him?"

There was no answer to that question—unless the pilot of the Kittyhawk was dead, and the plane was coming in of its own accord. Red brushed that idea aside as a ridiculous one. He and Jimmy went racing along the sun-baked landing strip in the wake of the plane. By the time they had taken a dozen strides, it happened.

The Kittyhawk dropped until its belly smacked against the landing strip to send up a swirling cloud of dirt and dust. Then it slithered over on left wing, crabbed the tip and dug a wide circular trench in the ground. Then, as though invisible ropes had been cut, the whole thing went cartwheeling end over end across the field. It burst into flame, but just before the flames showed, something popped out of the cockpit like a pea from a split pod. It was the pilot of the plane, and Randall's heart turned to ice as he saw the figure hit the ground and lay still.

"If he wasn't dead, he is now!" Randall gasped,

and put even more speed into his running legs.

Jimmy Joyce stepped up his pace, too, and together they reached the pilot. One glance at the bleeding, broken body and they both knew instantly that the pilot was beyond help.

"The poor guy," Jimmy said with a tightness in his throat. "I wonder why he flew her right in to the deck like that? He certainly couldn't have expected to get away with that kind of a belly landing."

"No, but I don't think he did it on purpose," Red Randall murmured as he took his eyes off the dead man and glanced at the burning wreckage some fifty yards away. "My guess is that he was wounded and passed out and fell against the stick at the last minute."

Jimmy Joyce nodded and then they both turned around to see a jeep come tearing down the landing strip. Major Pratt was at the wheel. He leaped out almost before he had braked the jeep to a stop. When he saw the dead pilot, anger and sorrow lined his face.

"You knew him, sir?" Red Randall asked quietly.

Major Pratt did not reply. He knelt down and almost reverently went through the pockets of the pilot's uniform. He found nothing—not even a lone match, or a handkerchief, or a crumpled cigarette package. When he rose slowly to his feet, Randall could see that his face was tight with rage.

"Yes, I knew him," he suddenly said, as though Randall had just asked the question. "Lieutenant Stone, and one of the best fighter pilots I ever had in my command. He's been missing for over a month. We had given him up for dead. The Japs must have caught him soon after he landed. Look. Wires or ropes did that. Not the crash. The dirty dogs!"

As the Major spoke the last he bent over and opened the front of the dead pilot's shirt. The man's chest was banded by a dozen deep red lines, each a good half inch wide. They were the marks left by tightly drawn wires or ropes.

Neither Randall nor Joyce could stop from

shuddering as they stared down at the horrible sight.

"Killing is too good for the Jap rats!" Red blurted out harshly. "We ought to catch them alive and burn them in oil. All of them!"

"But we have to catch them first," Major Pratt said pointedly.

"What did you mean, sir, that he must have been caught soon after he landed?" Jimmy asked with a frown. "Landed where? You mean you saw him forced down?"

"No, I don't mean that," the C.O. said with a shake of his head. "Stone was on a special solo mission. A native came into camp one day to say that there was a badly wounded American officer in his village down at Baniara, on Goodenough Bay. He said that the officer was dying, and had asked for a member of Intelligence to be sent to him. It took the native over two weeks to get through the jungles and mountains to us, and he was just about dead himself. It was useless to send any one back with him, but three or four very valuable men of Intelligence had been unreported for some time, and it was believed that this dying officer was one of them. Stone had served with Intelligence before transferring to the Air Forces, and he volunteered to fly to Baniara. He planned to land on the beach and walk to the native village and get the dying officer's statement."

Major Pratt nodded toward the plane that was now just a smoking mass of wreckage.

"That he put it down is proved by the fact that he came back in it just now," he said slowly. "Whether or not he reached the village and the dying officer, we'll probably never know. I have a feeling that he did. He probably knew that he was going to pass out, and tried his best to land and tell us his story before that happened. He lost, and so we'll never know what he had to tell us. The Japs must have caught him, but didn't find his plane. He escaped—or maybe the rats left him for dead—and he somehow managed to reach his plane and get it into the air. He was a great pilot, a great fighter, a great boy. Stay here a minute with him, while I go back and send out an ambulance."

The C.O. stared down at the dead man for a moment. His lips twitched, and he blinked his eyes once or twice. Then he walked silently over to his waiting jeep and drove down the landing strip to the camp.

"Just five minutes sooner, and he might have made it," Jimmy murmured. "What a rotten break for him!"

"And maybe for us, too," Red said soberly. "Maybe he had information that would mean plenty to American Command here on New Guinea. I wonder what it was."

Little did those two youthful air aces realize that already some of the strands of that web of mystery were being woven into their lives!

Chapter VI

MILNE BAY MISSION

RED RANDALL's wrist watch said exactly fifteen minutes after four o'clock in the afternoon. Just why he looked at his watch and made sure of the time, he did not know. Maybe it was because he was now taking part in the initial raids on Milne Bay, and because these raids might decide the fate of New Guinea, he wanted to establish the correct time so that he could look back on this day with a certain amount of accuracy in later life. That is, if there was to be any later life for him!

His lips twisted in a crooked smile as that last thought flashed across his mind. Getting jittery already, and Milne Bay still some thirty miles away? He ignored the question and glanced down at the shore line of New Guinea ripping along under his wings. Between him and the shore line were fifteen Yank bombers. Eight of them were B-26 Marauders, and seven of them were B-25 North Americans. They were carrying plenty of "eggs," and as Randall stared at them he breathed a silent prayer that every egg would hit smack on its intended target.

Taking his eyes off the light bombers, he looked at the formation of Kittyhawks and Airacobras, of which he and his plane were a part. Altogether there were twelve of them. Jimmy Joyce was just off Red's left wing tip. He looked that way, caught Jimmy's eye and grinned. Young Joyce grinned back and made the usual hand signs of greeting. Naturally all pilots were under strict orders to maintain radio silence on this mission, so hand signals between them had to take the place of the spoken word. In times gone by Red and Jimmy had done a lot of flying together in the same plane. Now it seemed just a little strange not to be able to chew the fat with Jimmy over the intercom.

Milne Bay, at the extreme southeastern tip of New Guinea, came sliding up over the horizon. Red suddenly felt an uncomfortable uneasiness. It was not fear, but rather a premonition that something unpleasant was about to happen.

From the air the Bay looked like a huge wedge driven into the tip of the island to form two forks of land. Hills lined three sides of the Bay, and as on most of New Guinea, the hills rose upward from the water's very edge. The thick tangled growth, which seemed to cover every square inch of ground, made it appear impossible for even a Jap to exist there.

As Randall looked down on the Bay, he saw three surface ships tracing faint wakes. They were moving out to sea to escape the Yank raiders which by now had been spotted. As though by magic a huge swarm of Jap Zeros came sweeping up out of nowhere. There were a good fifty of them.

"Well, there aren't a hundred of the rats," Randall muttered, as he made sure his guns were ready to fire. "That's something, anyway."

The fighters were above the bombers, and the Zeros were below them, screaming up for clean belly shots. That was not the way it should be, and long before the climbing Japs were within gun range, the Yank fighter pilots did something about the situation. As practically one plane, they nosed over and went tearing down through the bomber formation to get at the Japs. And get at the Japs they did. The very first dive by those Yank eagles sent eight of the Zeros hurtling down in flames, and three others went limping away with smoking engines.

Red had the savage satisfaction of seeing his victim explode in mid-air and disappear in a shower of wreckage. But eleven from fifty still leaves thirty-nine, and so in the bat of an eyelash the air under the bombers was filled with twisting and turning, gun-spitting Yank and Jap planes.

The bombers, though, did not take part in the scrap, save when their gunners pegged at a Jap or two who came within range. They drilled onward past the air battle toward their targets.

Whirling and belting and kicking his Kittyhawk all over the sky as he charged Zero after Zero, Randall tried to take out a split second now and then to see how the bombers were making out. It was difficult, however, to even take snap glances their way. Zeros seemed to ring him completely and it was as though he was continually flying through a huge net in the sky made up of crisscross tracer-bullet smoke. He did, however, get the chance to see great columns of black smoke mounting skyward around the edges of the Bay. And he saw that two of the Jap surface ships scooting out to sea were afire and apparently doomed. But that was all. There were too many Japs skipping about in the air to give him a chance to study details.

A roaring thunder was in his head, and his mouth and throat were bone dry. The muscles of his body ached from the recoil vibration of his guns, and his arms felt as heavy as lead from hauling and heaving his Kittyhawk about the sky. That Jap bullets had found his plane was evident from the little rows of holes that marked both his wings. Part of his glass hatch had "melted" away, too. And the compass and air-speed indicator on his instrument board were a shambles. However, the Allison in the nose still roared out its mighty song of power, and the Kittyhawk answered his every touch of the controls.

Bringing the Kittyhawk about in a dime turn, just after having shot a Zero's right wing clean off at the fuselage, Red glanced upward to see a second swarm of enemy planes streaking downward. For the first time he broke radio silence and barked into his mike.

"Zeros upstairs and coming down fast!" he called out. "Upstairs, and in the sun!"

He let that be his warning to the other Yank fighter pilots still in the air, and nosed his own plane up to meet the diving Japs. He knew that time was running out fast. It was a two hundred and twenty-five mile flight back to Port Moresby. That meant the fighters could spend no more than thirty minutes over the target. Then they would have to quit and head for home, if they expected to get home. It had been planned for the bombers also to spend no more than thirty minutes over their targets so that they would have the protection of the fighters on the way back. However, with this new batch of Jap wings screaming down it would be almost impossible for the bombers to head back for Port Moresby. And so, to give the now bombless bombers all the breaks possible, Randall sent his lone Kittyhawk ripping upward in a desperate effort to throw the Japs offstride.

It was something like trying to hold back the tide with his bare hands, but Randall did not weigh his chances of survival as he prop-clawed upward. Every second of time gained by the bombers in getting away from Milne Bay was a second in their favor. And every bomber saved was just another Sunday punch that General Mac-Arthur could throw at the Nips again.

"Yeah, maybe here goes nothing!" Red shouted somewhat crazily. "But I'll take one or two of you along with me. And how I will!"

Perhaps the Japs were tearing down too fast to pull out of their dives. Or perhaps they were so dumbfounded to see a lone Yank plane ripping up at them that they could not think straight for the first few seconds. Anyway, not a shot was fired at Randall's Kittyhawk. And then he had picked off the leading Zero, and was right up in the middle of the pack.

He thought he saw two more Japs tumble earthward, but he was not sure. It really did not matter, anyway. What did matter was that the Japs had pulled out of their diving charge, and all were striving frantically to gang up on him and shoot him to ribbons. However, as much as the odds were against him, there was one small thing in his favor. The Japs had only one target whereas he had many. Everything that whipped across his sights had to be Jap, and he just let fly at everything.

Suddenly he caught a glimpse of other Yank wings. He thought he saw Jimmy Joyce go piling down past him to pin a Zero cold. But when he took a second look the plane was too far below him to see its markings. Besides, two Zeros were cutting in at him, one from either side, and their savage cross fire was pounding into his engine. He instantly dropped the Kittyhawk sharply by the nose, and in practically a continuation of the maneuver, hauled it up and around in a wing-screaming climbing turn. That way he caught one of the Zeros and promptly shot it out of the sky.

And then it happened!

It was bound to happen sooner or later, and so he was not surprised or unduly alarmed when black smoke started to pour back from his engine and the Allison began to cough and sputter. Jap bullets had taken their toll as he had known they would sooner or later.

"Get down, fellow! Get down fast, and then bail out. You know how these rats like to shoot guys hanging in the air!" Red told himself.

The Japs had seen that he was hit and they came rushing in for the kill. Randall dropped his Kittyhawk by the nose and sent it streaking downward as Jap bullets pecked away at his tail. The Allison had quit altogether, and oily black smoke poured back through his shattered glass hatch to choke and half blind him. He grimly held the plane in its mad dive, however. When he was certain that land or sea was dangerously close, he eased up out of his dive, rolled the Kittyhawk over on its back, banged open the hatch wide, unfastened his safety harness, and let gravity pull his body down into thin air.

"Be seeing you, fellows, maybe," he mumbled. "Meanwhile, get a million of them!"

Chapter VII

BLACK LIGHTNING

As GRAVITY pulled Randall down out of the cockpit of his doomed Kittyhawk, he instantly slapped his right hand across his chest and took a firm grip on the rip-cord ring of his parachute pack. At the same time he twisted his head for a quick glance downward. A brief moment of wild panic was his, and then he saw that he was a good thousand feet above the New Guinea coast line. There was time for him to release his chute before his body hit earth or water.

He promptly yanked the rip-cord ring, and let his body go limp. As he did so, invisible hands seemed to reach down, catch hold of him, and jerk him back up toward the sky. Then he was swinging gently back and forth at the ends of his shroud lines, the air-filled chute spread out above him. An upward glance convinced him that there were no Jap Zeros tearing down to riddle him.

In fact, for the first few seconds as he searched the skies above him he did not see any Jap planes at all. That stunned him for a moment, and he was unable to understand it until he stared toward the horizon. Toward the south he could see columns of smoke rising up from the bombed Jap installations about Milne Bay. High in the air above the smoke were clusters of tiny dots twisting and turning like so many angry hornets.

He stared hard at those clusters of dots, and then sighed softly. He was pretty sure that they all represented Jap planes. That meant that the Yank fighters and bombers were on the way back to Port Moresby. And he could not see them because they were on the other side of the mountains.

"But how I must have drifted during the scrap!" he exclaimed and squinted at the towering columns of smoke. "Last thing I knew I was practically over Milne Bay. But now I'm miles and miles from the place. And *where*, I wonder!"

As he uttered the last, he took a tighter grip on the shroud-line straps and looked down past his dangling legs at the ground. He saw that he was heading straight for a narrow strip of white sandy beach. He was now low enough to tell that he would hit it squarely; there was no need to slip his chute to avoid landing in the jungle on one side of the beach or in the water on the other side.

"Thanks, Lady Luck, for another small favor," he murmured. "At least I'm not due for a good ducking, or a good scratching from that jungle growth."

Perhaps Lady Luck stopped smiling at him at the very last instant. Or perhaps it was one of those tricky little ground winds that play along any wooded shore line. Anyway, when he was still a dozen feet or so off the sand, his parachute silk suddenly jerked crazily to the side, twisted him around, and he hit the beach heavily on his side, knocking every bit of air from his lungs.

For awhile he seemed to be swimming about in a throbbing black mist. Then as he began to draw air into his aching lungs, the black mist faded away.

"My error, Lady Luck," he muttered as he pushed up onto his knees and pulled on the shroud lines to spill the air from the silk. "You kind of let me down that time!"

Quickly he unbuckled his chute harness, slipped out of it and gathered the shroud lines and the silk in his arms. Now that he was down on the ground, the usefulness of his parachute was by no means at an end. There were a hundred different uses he could make of the silk and shroud lines. For one thing, the chute could serve as his jungle tent at night. The shroud lines could be fishing lines, or they could be woven into a rope. A pilot's parachute is a life saver in many ways, and Red wasted no time in folding his up and tying the bundle with the shroud lines.

In the chute pack was a small first-aid kit, which contained among other things chlorinating

tablets for purifying drinking water, and sulfanila-
mide in case he was wounded. A handy sheath
knife was already slung at his belt, as was his
service automatic. His pack also contained a small
package of emergency rations that would sustain
him for several days, in the event he found it impossible to live off the land.

All in all he was not in such a bad way. He
guessed roughly that he was about twenty miles
or so up the shore from Milne Bay, and perhaps
two hundred and forty miles from Port Moresby as
the crow flies. But between him and Port Moresby
were the Owen Stanley Mountains.

Red peered at the jungle that stretched like a
solid lush green wall up and down the edge of the
beach. "Any Jap cutthroats in there?" he whispered to himself. "What shall I do next?"

He answered his last question with immediate
action. There was no telling when a Jap plane
might come tearing by overhead, and it was fool-
ish just to stand there in plain sight on the beach.
He moved closer to the edge of the jungle, found

a spot where there was shade, and squatted down to take further stock of the situation. Hundreds of thoughts came crowding into his mind. How did the raid make out? How many bombers did we lose? How many fighters? What about Jimmy? Did he catch a package, or was he on his way back to Port Moresby? Was he alive, or dead, or a force-landed victim like himself?

"Okay, skip it!" he grated at himself. "What happened, happened, and there isn't a thing you can do about it. Best thing right now is to concentrate on you."

Suddenly he stiffened and sat absolutely motionless, his breath locked in his lungs. At the edge of the jungle, about forty or fifty feet to his right, something had moved. It may have been an offshore wind moving a clump of jungle leaves. It may have been some jungle animal. It may have been something human. Could it have been a Jap patrol?

The thought made him shudder, and he slid his right hand up to his holstered service gun and undid the flap button. All the while he kept his gaze riveted on the spot where he had seen movement. He had the sudden urge to leap to his feet and dive deep into the jungle at his back, but he controlled the impulse. Perhaps his eyes had simply played him a trick. If there were Japs near by, they probably had not seen him, or they would be charging down the beach now. He convinced himself that to remain absolutely motionless was his best bet for the time being.

Five, and then ten, agonizing minutes dragged by. His leg muscles began to ache unbearably, and he was filled with the insane urge to let go with a yell at the top of his voice. Though he saw no further movement, he could sense more than ever the presence of something back in the jungle.

Could it be natives who had seen him come down by parachute, but were afraid to show themselves? Or were they head-hunters silently stalking their victim? He knew that there were a few head-hunting tribes in the wilds of New Guinea who still practiced their horrible art. What a sweet finish that would be! Shot down by a Jap into the waiting arms of some head-hunters! He tried to swallow, but his mouth seemed filled with cotton. Sweat started to trickle down his face, and he clenched the butt of his service gun so tightly that his hand ached.

Slowly the spell passed and was gone. His breath came easier and his heart ceased pounding. A wave of shame at his fear and weakness engulfed him. He had seen no further movement, and not a single sound had come out of the jungle all the time he had sat paralyzed on the sand. If he was going to let his imagination run away with him like this in the daytime, how could he endure the night?

"Easy does it, Red," he said quietly to himself and forced his taut and stiffened muscles to relax. "Get hold of yourself, boy. Lots of guys have force-landed, or bailed out, and got back to safety. You're not the first one. Pull up your socks, fellow, and start using your head for a change. A couple of hours more and it will be dark. Are you going to try to get your bearings, or just stick here and sit it out?"

Somehow the sound of his quiet firm voice removed the remaining tension within him. He stood up and stretched his legs, deliberately took his eyes off that spot in the jungle, and turned and stared out over the water. He saw only blue water, stretching clear to the horizon. There was not a sign of a single surface ship, not even the telltale smoke from a stack. He turned again and stared toward the southeast along the shore line. Milne Bay was in that direction, but because of the way the hills rose straight up from the shore line, he could not see the columns of smoke left by the Yank bombers. There were no planes aloft that he could see or hear. He could hear nothing but the soft lap of the waves breaking on the strip of beach, and the almost ringing silence behind him in the jungle.

He shrugged, and took a coin from his pocket. "Heads I work my way along to the right," he said and sent the coin spinning into the air. "Tails I start off to the left."

The spinning coin came down and hit the sand. He leaned over and took a look. It was heads. His eyes suddenly were attracted to something else in the sand a few feet away from the coin. It was a rounded object, bleached a dirty white by the sun and rain. Its smooth roundness was what puzzled and stirred his curiosity, and he impulsively reached down, dug away the sand and picked up the object.

He looked at it, caught his breath in a sharp gasp, and almost dropped it. The object was the skull of a dead Jap; he could tell by the buckteeth. Was it the skull of a Jap sailor washed up by the sea? Or was it a Jap airman who had bailed out and died where he fell? Or was it a Jap soldier who had run afoul of a tribe of head-hunters?

Somehow that last seemed the most likely. He did not know why he felt that way, but he did. Furious with himself for letting his thoughts run wild, he took it out on the Jap skull. He hurled it far out into the water, and then brushed his hands together to get rid of some clinging grains of sand.

"And stay there!" he muttered. "I only wish that all your rat brothers were with you."

With a nod for emphasis he turned to his right and started walking along the beach, keeping close to the fringe of the jungle. With every step he took he felt that unseen eyes were upon him. He could not shake off the feeling, and when he reached the point where the beach ended and the jungle came right down to the water's edge, there were beads of sweat on his face, and the palms of his hands were damp and clammy. He stopped and peered angrily at the jungle in front of him.

"Am I just naturally yellow?" he grated at himself. "Or is something going to happen, and I've got a premonition?"

He stood motionless a moment as though expecting an answer. Then he sighed, shrugged, and started pushing his way into the silent, ominous jungle. His idea was to follow the shore line until he came to the mouth of some stream or river. Then he would follow the river up its course. The reason for that, as had been explained to him by a pilot who had been forced to bail out over the wilds of New Guinea, was because all native villages, friendly or otherwise, were located on the banks of streams. And although he ran the risk of running into some unfriendly head-hunters, he knew that he had to find a native village if he ever expected to get out of his present predicament alive.

He did not stand one chance in a million of getting back to American-held ground on his own. The nearest bunch of Americans was many miles away. His only hope was to find some friendly natives, and get them to lead him back to the Port Moresby area. Following the shore line, he grimly fought his way through the heavy tangled growth inch by inch.

An hour passed. The sun was going down fast, and already the jungle was taking on the shadows of night. A great weariness pressed down upon him. Every step forward became both a mental and physical torture. A thousand unseen hands seemed to reach out and grab at his uniform, or catch him about the ankles and send him falling heavily to the ground. Panic tried to grip him in its spell.

"Take it easy, and keep your head," he kept telling himself over and over again. "Let yourself go, and you're sunk, kid. The jungle will get you cold if you do. Take it easy, and have a little rest. You've got lots of time. All the time in the world. Heck, nothing else but time is what you've got, fellow."

Talking aloud served to make his nerves less jumpy. It was a certain satisfaction to know he possessed the will power, the inner strength, to hold himself in check. He wondered if other fellows who had gone through this same ordeal had been filled with the same thoughts. Had it also been a double battle for them, too? A battle with themselves as well as with the jungle?

To take his mind off other things he continually asked himself questions like that, and tried to reason out the answers. And all the time he kept picking his way along the jungle-bordered shore line. Eventually, though, he could not go another step. He found the half-rotted trunk of a felled oleander tree, and sat down on it with a grateful sigh.

But no sooner did he become motionless than the unseen menaces of the jungle seemed to close in on him from all sides. And then, suddenly, he was certain that he saw swift, furtive movement in the tangled mass to his left.

He was not wrong! Black lightning seemed to streak out at him. He caught the flash of white teeth in a wide-eyed ebony face. Arms as big as tree trunks were raised up high, and the hand at the end of each arm gripped a long spear. He tried to duck back off the log and whip his service gun from his holster, but those streaks of black lightning were all over him before he could move a muscle. Instinctively he lashed out with his fist, and drove it straight into an ebony face. Pain shot all the way up his arm, and he had the feeling that he had driven his fist into a solid brick wall.

The next moment the jungle swam before his eyes and he sank into a dark void.

Chapter VIII

HUNTER'S PREY

THE PECULIAR sensation of falling gently down a long flight of carpeted stairs stirred Red Randall back to consciousness. He opened his eyes, but he could see nothing. Something was tied across his face and the smell of it gagged him. A dull throbbing ache filled his head, and it was several seconds before he became aware of the fact that his arms and legs were lashed tightly together. A moment later cold fear gripped him when he realized that his body was hanging from a pole like some trussed up animal being carried back to the hunter's camp.

The gently falling sensation changed to a violent jolting. He knew then that each end of the pole to which he was slung rested on somebody's shoulder, and he was jounced up and down every time a step was taken. Memory of black savages descending upon him returned, and he would have cried out impulsively, but the evil-smelling cloth over his face was bound so tight across his mouth that he could not utter a sound.

Audible now was a low chanting sound, a monotonous rhythm of the same two notes over and over again. Head-hunters! He had been trapped and caught by head-hunters. Of that he was certain, and the stark truth of it terrified him. It had not been his imagination after all; he had been watched from the depths of the jungle all the time. These savages had seen him land on the beach, had stealthily followed him through the jungle until he had sat down on the fallen tree trunk to rest. Then they had swooped down upon him and grabbed him.

What now? His captors were carting him to their village no doubt. How far was the village from here? How far had they carried him already? Was it night or day? How long had he been unconscious? He tried to cry out, tried to move his arms and legs, but found it impossible to do either. From head to foot he was conscious of a great numbing pain.

A dozen times Randall almost slipped back into unconsciousness. Why he did not let himself go back into that peaceful state angered him, and he called himself a fool. But it was as though consciousness was all he had left, and he clung to it tenaciously.

Suddenly the doleful chanting ceased. Now loud shouting and exclamations filled the air. Red's captors broke into a run; the jouncing became so violent that he almost passed out with pain. But he clenched his teeth hard and savagely refused to let go. And then without warning he was dropped. He hit something relatively soft, but the pole to which he was slung cracked down on his forehead. He lay as though dead, silently fighting off the wave of oblivion that strove to engulf him.

There was a great bustle of activity about him

now, but he was scarcely aware of it. Unintelligible chatter swept over and about him like storm waves. He half sensed, rather than felt, that he had been released from the pole. Then the evil-smelling cloth over his face was whipped away.

He blinked up through heavy jungle growth at a sun-filled blue sky. And then a collection of ebony faces blotted out the jungle growth and the sky. Big black eyes ringed by bloodshot whites stared down at him, and thick lips curled back to show gleaming white teeth in broad smiles. But they were not smiles of greeting to Red Randall, and he started to shout at them, only to find that a strip of rag was still tied across his mouth.

As he lay there helpless, the tribe of natives, both men and women, increased until it seemed a solid black wall was before him. Suddenly he heard the sound of an airplane engine. The blacks heard it, too, and they cringed as though in fear and turned their ebony faces toward the sky. For a brief instant a wild hope leaped up in Randall.

But it died even as it was born. He could tell from the sound of the airplane engine that it was not American or Australian. It was Jap—a Jap Zero.

This was confirmed a moment later when the plane streaked across the patch of sky that he could see. It was low enough so that he was able to see the red ball on the side of the fuselage. The natives saw it, too. They pointed upward, then turned and pointed their long black fingers down at him. They made harsh laughing sounds, nodded violently, and drew their fingers across their throats. It was then that Randall's greatest fear was realized. They thought him a Jap. They had mistaken him for a Jap. And they were indicating what was to be his fate. No doubt it was to be their revenge on the monkey men who were ravaging their homeland.

"No! No! I'm not Jap. I'm American! I'm your friend! Your friend!"

But he was only screaming the words in his mind, because it was utterly impossible for any sounds to come off his lips. He shook his head violently from side to side, but the natives only nodded their heads and laughed all the more.

Eventually, as though suddenly tiring of staring at their prize, the natives turned one by one and moved away, leaving only a little boy who seemed powerless to take his shoe-button eyes off Randall. A moment later a voice called out, and the boy, too, went scampering off. Randall tried to turn his head to see what he could of the place about him, but a bush no more than a foot from his head blocked his view of the village. And on his other side there was just jungle.

He closed his eyes hard and concentrated on counting slowly up to twenty-five. That helped him to relax somewhat and so he tried it again. His heart beat slowed down slightly, and he was able to think a bit more clearly. He was not dead yet. Could he hope that by some miracle his life would be spared?

"Steady, kid, steady!" he told himself. "Hang on and pray!"

But Red found it even difficult to pray. The sounds in the village set his thoughts spinning. How soon would the natives return? What were they doing now? Were they preparing for some sort of ceremony before they claimed the life of their victim?

"Easy, boy, easy!" he tried to check his looping thoughts. "Don't think. Don't let yourself think. It won't get you a thing. It will only make you feel worse."

Fortunately, there is a limit to the duration of any kind of shock, and after an hour or so Red was overcome by a sense of grim resignation. He was still alive, for that he could be thankful. The natives probably were waiting for someone. Red could not recall seeing any one who looked like the tribe's chief. Perhaps they were waiting for their chief. There was another hope, too. Perhaps before they killed him they would remove the gag from his mouth. Then he would be able to talk, and perhaps make them realize that he did not make the same sounds as the Japanese whom they obviously hated. He would draw the U. S. plane insignia on the ground, too. One of them might recognize it and convince the others that he was their friend and not their enemy.

A second, far less painful hour dragged by, and then suddenly from off in the distance he heard shouting. He paid little attention to it at first, but when the village natives began to shout back, a quiver went through him, and his heart again began to pound hard. Was that distant shouting what the villagers had been waiting for? It probably signaled the approach of someone. Could it be the tribe chief? He turned his head toward the shouting but he could see nothing. Then the sun moved into a clear patch of sky through the trees, and he was forced to close his eyes.

The shouting continued, and cold fear mounted within Red Randall. He tried desperately to wiggle and twist about and free himself of the lashings that bound his legs and arms, but steel bands could not have held him more firmly. He finally realized it was useless and lay gasping for breath, his head turned to shield his face from the hot sun as much as possible.

The shouting came closer. Then it died out completely and the air was filled with the chattering and jabbering of native talk. Red understood not a word that was spoken, but he guessed that the villagers were telling the newcomers about their prisoner. Soon he smelled the smoke of a cooking fire. Was this the beginning of the head-hunter's savage ceremony?

Chapter IX

NEW ARRIVALS

THE SOUND of many bare feet padding across the ground came to Red Randall's straining ears. Impulsively he exerted every ounce of his remaining strength to pry his arms free. But his efforts simply brought on intense pain and near-oblivion. Hot tears of bitterness and rage stung the backs of his eyes. To meet death at the hands of those whose homeland he had been fighting for was a bitter thought.

A shadow fell across his face and he opened his eyes to stare up at a black man who looked seven feet tall. Angry black eyes bored down into his. As they traveled down to his feet and back to his face again, they widened in amazement and chagrin. Without warning a voice choked out his name, and somebody dropped down beside him.

"Red! Red! My gosh, guy! What have they done to you?"

Everything began to swim before Red Randall's eyes. The evil-smelling rag was torn from his mouth and he suddenly realized that he was laughing uncontrollably. Was that Jimmy Joyce? Of course not, he was imagining things; he was going completely haywire.

But it had happened. It was true. It was Jimmy Joyce's arm about him, and it was Jimmy's other hand that was taking the bonds off his legs. And it was Jimmy's voice he could hear.

"Good gosh, Red, you look half dead, and you must be. Praise be I'm here. They thought you were a Jap, Red. Speak to me, Red. Say something! Are you all right, fellow? Are you hurt much? Say something, fellow!"

Red Randall tried to speak, but for the life of him he could not utter a single word. He could only stare unbelieving at Jimmy Joyce and at the seven-foot native who bent over and helped Joyce remove the strong vine lashings about his legs.

"Jimmy! Jimmy Joyce! You, fellow? I thought they were going to . . . to . . ."

The words came with a rush, and then he stumbled and faltered. Jimmy's arm about him tightened, and when he spoke there was an odd catch in his voice.

"Okay, Red, okay. Don't try to talk. Everything's okay now. The chief, here, speaks a little English. He would never have let this happen. He'll beat their heads together, if you tell him to. Here, Red, try to stand up. It'll help get the circulation started. I'll hang onto you. Don't bother talking, Red. Boy, what a going-over they must have given you."

Randall did not talk. It was effort enough to get slowly up onto his feet with Jimmy's help. When he finally stood upright a million pins and needles shot through his body. The ground spun around and around, and he would have fallen but for Jimmy's supporting arms about him. Gradually the spinning stopped, and the needles and pins disappeared. He sucked air into his lungs, swallowed hard, and looked at Jimmy intently.

Jimmy Joyce was a sight. His uniform was torn and ripped to shreds, his helmet and goggles were gone, and his face was a network of red welts and tiny scratches. But there was a grin on his lips, and a look in his eyes that suddenly made Randall want to give way to tears. Instead, though, he grinned back.

"Just guess how glad I am, Jimmy," he said. "Just try to, but you couldn't even come close. Now I know there are such things as miracles. One has just happened. But what about you, Jimmy? What about you?"

Before Joyce could say anything the big booming voice of the seven-foot native filled the air. He gave Randall a broad smile and poked a huge forefinger at him.

"My people say you a Jap," he said. "They no understand. Me understand you no Jap. Your friend, he no Jap, too. My people catch. They kill you for Jap. But no more. Me tell them you no Jap.

You friend. White friend. My people sorry. They get much food. You eat. Everybody eat. Everybody feel good. Kill Japs. No kill white friend. Me understand. Me go Port Moresby long ago. Me know white friend good friend."

The big black turned on his heel, threw up a hand, and roared at the villagers. They all grinned and violently nodded their heads. Red grinned back at them to let them know that all was forgiven as far as he was concerned. The tribe chief motioned to Jimmy and Red and walked over toward a cluster of kunai grass huts built on the edge of a wide stream which Randall now saw for the first time. The big chief entered the largest of the huts and squatted on the floor. He beat his big hands together and roared out in his native tongue. Randall and Jimmy squatted down as the big black pointed to a spot about five feet in front of him.

"You make talk. Food come soon. Everybody make talk. Me help. My people help. You good white man friends. You make talk."

With that the tribe chief got to his feet again and walked out of the hut.

"Is that an old head-hunter's custom?" Red asked as the big fellow disappeared. "And are they head-hunters?"

"They are, or rather they used to be, he told me," Jimmy replied. "They don't go in for that kind of thing any more. But tell me what happened to you, Red. Are you all right now? I had the scare of my life when I saw you all tied up."

"Scare of *your* life?" Randall said with a laugh. "I'm the one who had the scare, pal, and I don't mean maybe. You'd be ashamed of me, Jimmy, for some of the thoughts I had. I'm telling you, it was really tough. I sure thought that I'd come to the end of the line, and I was so scared I could hardly breathe. How do you happen to be here, though?"

"You tell me your story first. My experience was very ordinary," young Joyce grinned.

Randall shrugged and gave Jimmy a detailed account of his unpleasant experience.

"I guess they must have camped out some place last night, as it must have been midmorning when I finally woke up," he finished up. "Anyway, I haven't the slightest idea where we are. But the sooner I can get away from here the better I'll like it, even if they all are very sorry and so forth. Now how about your story, Jimmy? You bailed out, too?"

"And in a hurry," Joyce said with an emphatic nod. "Darn near too much of a hurry, too. Lucky I didn't break my neck. There were half a dozen Japs practically flying into me. You see, I'd spotted your plane near the end of the scrap, and saw the whole darn sky around you full of Zeros. I cut over to give you a hand. The Japs didn't like the idea and they came at me in force. I picked off a couple but there was a whole swarm of them. Not all of them could miss at the range, and not all of them did. I don't think there was a square inch of my Kittyhawk that they didn't hit. Missed me completely, though. Pardon me while I rap on some wood."

Jimmy paused, tapped the knuckles of his right hand against his head, and grinned.

"They put me out of that scrap for keeps, but the bombers had started back by then," he continued presently. "My engine caught fire, and it was going to be curtains for me if I didn't do something quick. The darn Japs were having a field day, and I don't mean perhaps. I risked sticking with the ship a little longer and dove right down away from them. I guess they didn't expect that. They expected me to bail out and let them have more fun. Anyway, they didn't come down after me. I pulled out at about five hundred, or so I thought. It was more like three hundred, and believe me my chute opened just in time. It no sooner opened and checked my fall than I was down in the thickest, thorniest section of jungle on New Guinea. I'll cover any bet anybody wants to make that it wasn't. Just try to imagine going down feet first into a great big pile of broken bottles and barbed wire, and you'll have some idea of what it was like."

Jimmy Joyce paused again, gave a little shake of his head, and blew air out past his lips.

"I didn't think I'd have a patch of skin or a thread of cloth on me before I stopped," he said. "The chute silk fouled of course, and there I was hanging between two trees with the ground still a good twenty feet below me. Well, for awhile I didn't do anything, I was too winded and exhausted. If a jungle animal had come along I would have been his meal for the taking. Even my gun holster had been ripped off; I never did find it."

"And you say your experience was very ordinary?" Randall said as Joyce paused for breath again.

"Well, I guess it really was the usual thing in these parts," Jimmy said with a shrug. "That doesn't mean I liked it, though. Or that I won't remember it for a long time, either. As I said, I dangled there under my fouled chute not caring what happened next. Eventually I got some sense and decided to do something about the situation.

I got myself swinging, and grabbed another branch of one of the trees. I wiggled up onto it, slipped off my chute harness, and then started down to the ground. I practically fell most of the way down that tree, but the ground where I finally lighted was soft, so I didn't break any bones. It took me over an hour to get down, believe it or not."

"And it felt kind of good, didn't it?" Red Randall chuckled.

"Almost got down on my hands and knees and kissed it, I was so glad to feel it under me," Jimmy said gravely. "Well, I didn't have the faintest idea where I was, or even which side was up, you might say. The jungle was just four green walls about me, and a solid green ceiling above me. I couldn't see a single patch of the sky. It wasn't exactly dark down there on the ground. There was a weird, pale sort of light that made it possible for you to see things. But all you could see was jungle and more jungle."

"I know just what you mean!" Randall declared.

"As far as I'm concerned, they can blow up this island and sink the whole works, once we've kicked the Japs off."

"A better idea would be to sink it with them all on it," Jimmy corrected. "Anyway, there I was, with no idea which way was north, south, east, or west. I didn't know whether to start walking in any old direction, or to climb back up that tree and try to sleep out the night. Before I could make up my mind, up pops the chief and some of his men. To see them appear out of nowhere scared ten years off my life. I thought I was a goner, too, then. They had their spears all cocked, and nobody was smiling. In a way, I'm darn glad I was paralyzed with fright. If I hadn't been, I might have been fool enough to start running. When they came closer, the chief grinned and babbled something to his men. 'You good white friend, you no Jap,' he said to me. And you can bet your sweet life that as soon as I could move my tongue I told him that he was dead right!"

Young Joyce stopped talking, and drew a hand across his scratched forehead.

"Nothing like what you went through, Red," he said with a little laugh, "but it was plenty enough for me, I can tell you. Well, with the ice broken, so to speak, we started to palaver back and forth as much as his knowledge of English would permit. Kagi, he told me his name was, said that they were out on a Jap hunt. He said that they once had a village some miles from here and one day Jap pilots came along and strafed and bombed the tar out of the place. Almost half of his tribe was killed. They started hating Japs that day, and ever since they've been taking their revenge on any force-landed Jap they could find, and any Jap soldiers they could ambush. Kagi says they've gotten quite a bunch of them."

"One of whom was me, almost," Randall said and swallowed hard.

"Almost," Jimmy said and grinned. "Don't be angry with them, though, Red, even if they did give you quite a going-over. I was the first white man any of them, with the exception of Kagi, had ever seen. Our planes haven't been over this area much, and so anybody who came down was Jap to them. None of those who jumped on you spoke or understood English. You were just another Jap to them, and they lugged you back to this village so that the whole tribe could see you get the works. That's the way they do it, Kagi told me. Every member of the tribe lost some relative in that first Jap raid, so they all share in the revenge."

"Well, I'm sure in favor of that custom!" Randall said with emphasis. "If it had been a case of every man for himself, I wouldn't be here. I take it, though, you came down quite some distance from this village? You spent the night in the jungle?"

"With Kagi and his men," young Joyce said with a nod. "And quite an experience, too. We slept in some trees, and it wasn't bad at all. And the food they dug up didn't taste too bad. As soon as it was light we started back. I couldn't see how we could possibly force our way through the jungle, but Kagi and his boys certainly know their stuff. They followed trails I wouldn't have been able to see if one had up and hit me in the face. However, I was plenty tired by the time we reached here. And then I saw you."

"And I'll never again experience such a moment of joy and thankfulness as the moment when I saw you. Say what you will, I'll never . . ."

Randall did not finish the last. He cut himself off when he saw Jimmy Joyce staring wide-eyed past him. He turned around, and his own eyes instantly popped. Led by Chief Kagi, half a dozen tribesmen were approaching with wooden bowls filled to overflowing with food. They came into the hut and set the bowls on the mat floor. There was sago, and corn, and taro roots, and wonder of wonders, watermelon! Just looking at the array of food made Randall ravenously hungry.

"Now I've seen everything!" he exclaimed. "Don't ever let anybody tell you, Jimmy, that the day of miracles is past. It isn't. It's right here now, and how!"

Chapter X

PLANS FOR A JOURNEY

A FEAST that thoroughly satisfied both Red Randall and Jimmy Joyce was but the beginning of native hospitality. Kagi, chief of the New Guinea tribesmen, and the two youths were the only ones who ate. The other natives stood at a respectful distance and watched them gravely. Whenever a bowl became empty, one of them would spring forward, rush away with it, and in no time at all return with it filled to overflowing again.

While he ate, Randall studied the natives and silently admired their strong, healthy bodies. He noted that several of them wore strips of his chute silk tied about their jet-black hair. A couple of them had items of his personal equipment stuck inside their loin cloths. He saw the cover of his first-aid pack, and some of his K ration package. He did not see his knife or his service automatic, however. They had stripped him of everything he had, believing him to be a Jap and fair game. Well, they were welcome to their loot as payment for what Red hoped they would be able to do for Jimmy and himself, which was lead them safely back to the Port Moresby area.

When the feast was over, Kagi spoke for the first time. He shouted in his native tongue and clapped his enormous hands together. Two native women stepped forward, each carrying a small bowl in her hands. Red groaned inwardly, for he was sure that he could not possibly eat another mouthful. But it was not food that the native women carried. Each bowl contained a blackish liquid that looked like used engine oil. One of the women started to smear the stuff over Red's cuts and bruises, while the other administered the same treatment to Jimmy Joyce.

To his astonishment, Red found the ointment soothing beyond description. The aches, the smarting, and the stinging left his face and hands in a flash. When he glanced at Jimmy he saw that he was more than pleasantly surprised, too.

"Boy, if we could take the formula of this stuff back home, we'd make millions in nothing flat!" Red exclaimed.

"A little on the sticky side, but it gets my money," young Joyce replied. "I was beginning to feel pretty uncomfortable and worried, too. Among other things, I lost my first-aid kit. And I see you gave yours away, eh?"

"Yes, I gave it away," Randall said, catching Joyce's meaning. "Let's let it ride that way."

"Maybe it's best that we do," Joyce murmured, and then shook his head at the native woman who was getting set to smear him all over again. "That's fine, and thank you very much," he said. "No. No more. Fine. I'm okay now."

Kagi grunted something and the two native women looked a trifle reproachfully at their "patients," picked up their bowls and went away.

"That good!" Kagi spoke in English. "Make you

sick no more. Now we talk. We talk war. Me, Kagi, no like Japs. Kill my people. Me kill them. Japs no good. Where Kagi go find Japs?"

The tribe chief leaned forward and stared earnestly at Red and Jimmy out of his big black eyes.

"What name this place?" Randall asked and made a sweeping movement with his right hand. "Good white man friends lost. Want to go Port Moresby. How long? You take us we give you many presents."

Kagi scowled and shook his head.

"Presents no good," he said. "Me want find Japs. Port Moresby longa, longa way. Many days. Maybe not find. Maybe die. No good."

"You know place Baniara?" Jimmy Joyce suddenly asked. "That longa, longa way, too?"

The tribe chief suddenly beamed all over his black face.

"Me know Baniara!" he cried. "Got brother. His tribe have village no longa Baniara. Two days maybe. Good white friends live my brother. Kill Japs longa time."

Both Joyce and Randall were stunned.

"Good white friends in your brother's village?" Red asked. "You mean soldiers? White soldiers?"

"Soldiers?" Kagi repeated with a frown, pronouncing the word so that it sounded like "soldos."

"Yes," Randall said, and went through the motions of firing a rifle. "Men go like this! Bang-bang-bang! Lots of Japs die. White soldiers. Like me. Like my friend."

Kagi had started to beam and nod his big head, but he suddenly stopped and frowned in puzzlement.

"No white man-birds Baniara," he said. "White men shoot on ground. Go into bush, into jungle, find Japs. Come back my brother's village. My brother speak with me. I visit. One day longa white man-bird come. No good. Japs find. My brother no see white man-bird no more."

"Red!" Jimmy Joyce breathed fiercely. "Do you know what he means? He means that pilot, Stone, we saw crash and kill himself. I'll bet you anything!"

"No bet, because I think you're right," Red replied, as excitement rippled through him. Then turning to Kagi, he said, "White soldiers shoot on ground, good. White man-bird shoot in air, good, too. How many white soldiers shoot on ground at Baniara?"

Kagi frowned some more and Red could not tell whether he was puzzling over the meaning of his words or trying to figure out the answer. Presently he grunted and started opening and closing his big hands, each time sticking his fingers up straight.

"Many white soldiers," he said, and stuck to his own pronunciation of the word soldiers. "Many like my people. Many guns."

Both Red and Jimmy were too astonished by Kagi's words to speak for a moment or two. Troops at Baniara? It seemed incredible. Port Moresby was the only part of New Guinea still held by General MacArthur's forces. True, there were a few isolated patrols moving about in the jungle, striving to harass Jap forces and disrupt supply and communication lines. But they were simply jungle commando raids on a very small scale. These patrols consisted of fifteen or twenty men, but Kagi had said there were as many white troops at Baniara as he had villagers. Neither Randall nor Joyce had counted the natives in the village, but they were both certain that the number totaled more than one hundred.

"How long white soldiers at Baniara?" Randall asked. "Longa time before war? Know how they got there?"

"Kagi know," the chief replied and solemnly nodded his big head. "My brother tell Kagi. White soldiers come rain go. Come boat. Bad storm. Boat no good. Make big noise. Go under water. White soldiers get small boats. Come shore. Many sick. Many die. Jap man-birds come. My brother and his men give help. Take white soldiers, guns, where Jap man-birds no find. With my brother kill Japs.

"No more Japs this place. Kagi and men go my brother. Kill many Japs. That good."

"I guess that means Port Moresby is out, but definitely," Red murmured to Jimmy as Kagi gave a violent nod of his bushy head and lapsed into silence. "I don't know what to make of his story. Do you suppose one of our troop transports was sunk off Baniara, and some of them managed to get to shore and are now operating out of Kagi's brother's village?"

"It sure sounds like that to me," Jimmy said with a nod. "But according to what Major Pratt said, that native runner told him there was just one Yank officer at the village, and dying. If there were others, why didn't he say so? The Major could have arranged for supplies to be flown to them."

"These natives have queer ways," Randall replied with a shrug. "Maybe that dying officer sent him to tell Intelligence where he was, and the native took him literally. Nobody asked him, so he didn't say that others were there, too. I wonder if Stone found out, and that's why he tried to get down in such a hurry?"

"Maybe, but I don't think we'll ever know for sure," young Joyce sighed. "I think we should look into this Baniara business, Red. Kagi won't take us back to Port Moresby, so let's get him to take us to his brother's village. If there are some Australians and some of our boys there, we'll at least be two more to help out."

"If Kagi intends to join his brother, I'm certainly not going to let him leave us behind," Red said.

Randall turned to Kagi who sat staring unseeing into space. "When you go Baniara join brother?" he asked.

The big native blinked, rolled big eyes Red's way and regarded him in solemn silence for a moment.

"Kagi go sometime," he rumbled deep in his throat. "Rains come, go, Kagi and people go. Lots of food this place. Kagi tired. Go brother's village two moons maybe."

"Oh-oh, not so good!" Jimmy breathed softly. "That could mean weeks and maybe months from now, Red. Maybe he'll take us there first, and come back to get his people later."

"War no good," Randall said to the chief. "Make everybody tired. Good for Japs, though. They like white soldiers tired. Kill sooner, before other white soldiers come. That bad. That very bad. My friend and I want to go your brother's village and help white soldiers kill Japs. White soldiers want us very much. You take us to your brother's village and all white soldiers be your friend, good friend, longa, longa time. Give you anything you want. Give you gun maybe. You take us your brother's village, yes?"

Red's sales talk did not impress Kagi. As Red finished, Kagi blinked sleepily, and yawned loudly.

"White soldiers Kagi's friend now, alla time," he said. "Kagi and people go my brother's village by and by. Get gun then. Kill Japs. Kagi take you good white man-birds when Kagi go with people to my brother's village."

"And that seems to be that," Randall muttered

as he turned to Joyce. "No soap. The guy has a stubborn streak, it would appear."

"Well, anyway, your pep talk sure left him cold," Jimmy said with a grimace. Then his face suddenly brightened and he added quickly, "Let me take a whirl at him, Red. I've got an idea."

"Help yourself, kiddo, the floor is yours," Randall grunted. "I hope your idea works. I'll go nuts if I have to hang around here for any length of time."

"You wouldn't be the only one," Joyce echoed and leaned toward Kagi. "You no go longa time your brother's village would be bad, much bad, Kagi," he said earnestly.

The big native chief blinked at him and scowled.

"When Kagi go my brother's village good for my brother's people," he said stoutly. "How be bad?"

"Much, much bad," Jimmy replied gravely. "Our white man chief tell us many, many Japs come over water in big boats with many guns soon. Big boats shoot big guns at your brother's village. Many, maybe all your brother's people die. White soldiers all die, too. Nobody to help. Jap soldiers come on land, burn village, and kill anybody they find. You go brother's village longa time, find nothing there. All gone. All die. Many Japs catch you. You die, too. Me die. My friend die. Whole country belong Japs. No good."

An expression of awe spread over Kagi's face, and then it slowly changed to one of anger. The veins stood out on his neck, his eyes became as big as dinner plates, and he thumped his two clenched fists against each other.

"You speak bad words not so?" he cried. "You say Japs kill my brother, not so?"

Jimmy Joyce had to swallow a couple of times before he spoke. For a moment he had been afraid that Kagi was going to slam a fist into his face.

"Yes, it is so, Kagi," he said. "White friends know that many, many Japs will come in big boats with big guns. We go your brother's village quick and you tell brother to hide in new village. Japs come and no find. Japs look, and we catch them and kill. Others get big scare and maybe go back to their big boats and sail away. Your brother no die. His people no die. We no die. Only Japs die. Longa time go your brother's village much bad. Go quick, now, much good. We warn your brother and white soldiers. You savvy, Kagi?"

The native chief seemed to be having a battle within himself, for he did not speak for two full minutes. Then with a yell he shot up onto his feet, and both Jimmy and Red held their breaths.

"Japs kill my brother, no good!" he roared. "No kill. Japs die. We go my brother. I go make talk my people. Get food. You wait. Sun straight up, we go!"

With no more disturbance than a hurricane would cause, Kagi went charging out of the hut bellowing at the top of his voice in his native tongue. Behind him Red Randall and Jimmy Joyce sat wiping beads of cold sweat from their foreheads.

"You sure sold him a bill of goods, pal!" Randall

breathed softly. "But what about when he finds out that it's a phony? Any special place you'd like the pieces sent?"

"I'm getting us to Baniara, aren't I?" Joyce snapped, though his eyes looked troubled.

"You sure are!" Randall admitted. "But I had in mind when we *get* there."

"Okay, I'll go tell him I was just kidding," Jimmy said and started to get up.

Randall grabbed his arm. "Hey, no!" he gasped. "I was just giving you a rib, Jimmy."

"Think I would have told him?" Jimmy grinned as he sat down again. "Don't be silly! I'd have told him anything to get him to take us there. Matter of fact, I didn't muss up the truth too much. Jap reinforcements are coming down to New Guinea every day. Like as not one batch of them is bound to come ashore at Baniara sooner or later. And after all, how can he prove that I'm wrong?"

"He can't, so let's skip it," Randall said. "You did okay. The main thing is to get him to take us to Baniara, and it looks like you've fixed that for us. My only worry now is what the trip will be like."

"We'll find out soon enough," Jimmy murmured. "Here comes Kagi, and he looks all packed and ready to start right now."

Chapter XI

ENEMY PATROL

LOW-SWEEPING tree branches formed a continuous arch across the narrow, deep New Guinea stream. At times the stout vine-lashed bamboo raft floated along serenely in the direction of Baniara; at times it pitched and tossed like a chip of wood in a raging gale.

Red Randall and Jimmy Joyce, with Chief Kagi and five of his tribesmen, had started the journey downstream early the evening before. It was the natives who had made the raft when the party, after traveling seven hours from the native village, had come to the river. Their knives had gone through four-inch thick bamboos as through sticks of butter. In no time at all, the raft, strong enough to withstand the toughest stretches of the stream, was ready.

The moment Randall and Joyce climbed aboard, they fell into a deadlike sleep. The seven-hour "hike" through the steaming jungle had sapped their strength completely. The natives had carried the food and some bags of gifts which Kagi was taking along for his brother. Red and Jimmy were burdened with nothing save a jungle knife which Kagi had given to each of them. But just keeping up with the natives had been a tough enough job for them. The jungle was new to them, and where the natives took two steps to avoid an obstacle in their path, Red and Jimmy had to take half a dozen, and often ended up by falling anyway.

Although the sticky black magic smeared on his skin had relieved the pain and smarting of his cuts and bruises, Red had not had enough rest to undertake this exhaustive journey. He complained not a word, though, and struggled to keep from showing his fatigue. It was now close to the sunset of another day and he still lay fast asleep on the raft. Jimmy had awakened a few moments ago.

"Long time to brother's village, Kagi?" he asked.

The chief, who sat at the front end of the raft and continually grunted orders at the men guiding the raft along, turned around slowly and shook his head.

"Him up there now," he said, pointing a forefinger at the slivers of sunshine that filtered through the arch of branches. "When him much low we come my brother's village. Rains make river fast. We go quick time my brother's village."

"And that will be very much okay by me," Randall murmured, opening his eyes and rolling over to a more comfortable position. "There's nothing like a nice boat ride on the river *if* you can pick your river."

"*And* your boat!" Jimmy interjected. "These bamboo poles are putting stripes in my hide that'll never smooth out again. Five or six hours more, and we can say finish to this journey."

"It sure has been an experience," Randall said, "and I'll be glad when we reach Baniara. Just the same I'd say we're two very lucky guys. We get shot down and drop right smack into a bucket of luck."

Jimmy Joyce grinned and nodded absently.

"I wonder how many troops there really are at Baniara," he said presently, "and if any of them are our boys. It would be something, wouldn't it, if we could clear up that mystery about the pilot Stone?"

"Yes, it would. I'd like to be able to write and tell his folks about it some day. It helps, I've always thought, for a fellow's folks to know the details, to know not only where but how their boy died. If I ever caught one I'd like somebody to tell my Dad how. . . ."

Red stopped short, bit his lip hard, and gave an apologetic shake of his head. The sudden whiteness of Jimmy Joyce's face had stopped his thoughtless talk instantly. No one would be able to tell Jimmy's father anything about his son. He had died that terrible December Sunday at Pearl Harbor aboard the ill-fated *U. S. S. Arizona.* Red's father, too, had been at Pearl Harbor that day. Though his life had been spared, he would never fly again at the head of his fighter squadron. It would be a long time before he walked again. But he was alive, and Jimmy's father was dead.

"I'm sorry, Jimmy boy," he said softly. "Just leave it to Big Mouth Randall to stir up memories that hurt. I'm sorry, Jimmy."

"Don't be sorry, Red, that's silly," young Joyce said quietly. "You have a perfect right to talk about your Dad, fellow. If you do catch one, and if I see it, I promise to tell your father how it all happened. I know he'd want to know. As for my Dad, well . . . he'll know all about it right at the time. That's the way I feel about it, Red. He knows about me even now, this very minute. So don't feel bad. Nothing stirs up unhappy memories for me, Red, not since I've taught myself how to think about Dad."

Randall could not speak for a moment. He was

too choked up with emotion. He reached out and pressed Joyce's hand.

"You're a grand guy, Jimmy," he finally managed to say. "You're the grandest guy in the world. They just don't make them any better."

Jimmy flushed and grinned broadly.

"Well, for a guy who claims to be an observing cuss," he chuckled, "it certainly took you long enough to find that out!"

"Yes, one grand guy," Randall muttered, "but he could do with a sock on the jaw every now and then to teach him to be respectful to his betters!"

They both laughed and the somberness and tension of the moment was gone. But above their laughter Kagi's voice came back to them like the hiss of a whip.

"No sound! Make no sound! We stop!"

The last was quite true. Randall and Joyce suddenly realized that the natives had guided the raft into the bank and were holding it motionless, while all of them crouched like so many huge panthers set to spring. Their eyes were wide and the bloodshot whites showed large and clear. Every one was staring straight at Kagi, waiting for the tribe chieftain to speak. Randall leaned forward.

"What's wrong, Kagi?" he whispered. "What do you hear?"

Kagi looked at him, and through him, and did not speak. For a long minute not a man on that raft moved. And then Kagi said something in a low voice to one of his men. The man nodded, took his wicked-looking jungle knife out of his loin cloth, and stole off the raft and up into the jungle to disappear as swiftly and as silently as a black shadow.

Everybody remained silent and motionless after the native had disappeared. Presently Kagi cocked his head to one side, threw it back as though sniffing the steaming jungle air, and finally turned around and snaked back over the raft to Randall and Joyce.

"We stop," he whispered. "Maybe Japs close. By next turn. We hear. We smell, too. Maybe Japs."

Red and Jimmy exchanged glances, then stared hard at Kagi.

"Japs?" Jimmy asked. "Many Japs? Can you tell? Maybe we shouldn't just stay here and wait. It might be a force of them working their way upstream."

"And we haven't any guns," Randall said, regretting that he had not demanded the return of his service gun.

"We find out," Kagi said bluntly. "Japs no move. Kagi can tell. Maybe Jap camp. Maybe Jap manbird. Him find out. Come back tell me. One Jap, two Japs, many Japs—we kill all Japs. Japs no good."

It was hard for Randall to stifle the groan that rose up in his throat. It was plain to see that Kagi was obsessed with the idea of killing Japs. That it might be a fair-sized patrol, equipped with machine guns, rifles, and hand grenades, did not seem to occur to Kagi. A few Japs, or a lot of them, it was all the same to him. He intended to kill them all.

"Give with the old sales talk, Jimmy," Red said out of the corner of his mouth so quickly that the chief could not follow his words. "Our friend's all hot to make an umpchay out of himself. A little on the utsnay side. Give out but good. You're his pal."

Jimmy Joyce did not reply to Red. He turned his head and smiled at Kagi. The big native grinned back.

"We kill Japs," he murmured. "Japs no good!"

"All Japs no good, Kagi," Jimmy said softly. "But Japs no fools. You savvy?"

"Kagi savvy," the chief assured him. "Why Japs no fools? Japs fools come our land."

"Sure they were fools to come here, Kagi," Jimmy said. "But the Japs have learned things. Fear has made them learn things. They scared of Kagi and his people. They learn things. They be careful or Kagi and his people will kill them. You savvy?"

"Me savvy Kagi and his people kill Japs," the chief replied. "You say word, scared, me no savvy."

"You and your people have killed so many Japs, Kagi," young Joyce began but felt that he was simply getting into deeper and deeper water, "that Japs no let you catch them. No go into jungle just one, two, three Japs. Many Japs, so they will be strong. With many guns to shoot. Kagi and his people have no guns. Jungle knife no good if many Japs have guns. Kill you before you get close, and then . . ."

Jimmy let the rest slide as Kagi stubbornly shook his bushy head.

"Japs no hear Kagi come close," he said. "Kagi make no sound. No sound like night. Japs die. No sound. Like snake in water."

"My error, Jimmy," Red murmured. "Better give it up, kid. The lad is spoiling for a scrap, that's all. Let's just hope it isn't Japs up ahead."

Kagi missed completely the meaning or sense of Randall's words, for he suddenly beamed on him and nodded his head violently.

"Kagi kill all Japs," he said. "Good white friends no die. Kagi kill all Japs. Kagi show!"

"Sure, Kagi," Red said and grinned at him. In an undertone he added, "But make it good, big boy. Be sure and make it good."

That seemed to end the conversation. Kagi snaked his way back to the front of the raft and squatted there, head cocked a little to one side. Randall and Joyce exchanged worried looks. There was nothing they could do now. The affair was in Kagi's hands, and all they could do was hope for the best.

Ten, fifteen, twenty minutes dragged by. A black shadow moved on the bank to the left. The tribesman who had slipped into the jungle returned aboard the raft just as quietly as he had left. He moved directly to Kagi and murmured unintelligible sounds in his ear. Then he held up the five fingers of one hand and three fingers of the other. Kagi's dark face seemed to light up with wild excitement. Red and Jimmy groaned softly, for it was not hard to guess the meaning of the eight fingers and the elation on Kagi's face.

"He's mad!" Randall breathed fiercely. "That

lad has found eight Japs up ahead, and Kagi is tickled pink with the news. We've got to knock some sense into his thick head. Why, there isn't even a water pistol among us!"

"I know, and I suddenly don't feel so good," Jimmy mumbled. "I'm afraid we can't stop him. Only a Jap slug is going to cool down his crazy yen to fight. He just doesn't understand."

Randall sighed sadly but before he could say anything, Kagi moved back to them, looking like a little boy who is seeing his first Christmas tree.

"Japs no longa from this place," he stated avidly. He held up eight fingers. "So many. You wait. No let raft go away. Kagi come back soon. All go my brother's village. Tell my brother how Kagi kill Japs. My brother be much happy. All have big feast. Good."

"No, bad, Kagi!" Randall spoke rapidly. "Much better kill Japs tomorrow. Japs got guns. You have only knives. No get close Jap guns with only knives. They shoot, bang, bang, bang! Kagi no see his brother no more."

The native's eyes blazed up in a look of utter scorn. He snorted and shook his head violently.

"No Japs kill Kagi!" he boasted angrily. "Kagi kill Japs much other times. Good. Kagi say you wait. No leave raft."

"Kagi wait short time to listen white friend?" Jimmy interrupted with the most disarming smile he could muster. "White friend have thought. Your brother like to kill Japs, yes?"

Kagi frowned at him, then nodded.

"Good," Jimmy said. "We near your brother's village. You kill Japs and tell him, maybe he get angry with you. Angry you no go straight his village and tell him where Japs camp. Don't you see, it's . . ."

"Talk no good," Kagi cut in, scowling. "Kagi kill Japs soon. Much soon. Watch raft or Kagi get mad. So!"

With a nod of his big bushy head, Kagi turned away, muttered to the other tribesmen, and all six of them slipped soundlessly off the raft to the stream's bank and disappeared in the jungle.

"What a sweet mess this turned out to be!" Randall whispered. "At least we should have insisted on going along. Brave guys with no brains sure give me a pain."

"Maybe they'll get away with it," Jimmy murmured with a shrug. "Maybe we underestimate their cunning. I guess they've had plenty of practice against the Japs."

"Sure, grabbing Nip pilots that force-landed or bailed out!" Randall muttered. "But it must be a patrol up ahead. Nips with guns who know what the jungle is all about. Maybe Kagi will get a couple of them, but machine-gun bullets will get him and his men just like that. If Kagi misses fire and the Japs come piling around that bend in the river, I don't want to be caught sitting here. I think we should tie up this thing and hide out on the bank. We're like clay pigeons in a shooting gallery here."

"I agree with you one hundred per cent," Jimmy said firmly. "Let's go. Kagi wants us to watch the raft. Well, we'll watch it from the river bank. And if he and . . ."

That's as far as Jimmy got. At that instant the jungle seemed to tremble with high-pitched screams. But the screams did not shock and stun them half as much as the yammer of machine-gun fire which followed.

"Kagi kill Japs, nuts!" Randall cried. "He's probably full of lead right now. And we'll get the same if we don't get out of here fast."

A second blast of machine-gun fire chattered through the jungle up ahead. Both youths fairly threw themselves off the raft and up onto the river bank. They paused just long enough to secure the raft to a tree root with a length of vine. Then they wiggled some distance through the jungle, and stooped to hug the ground and strained their ears for the slightest sound.

Chapter XII

WHITE MAN'S WAY

For two or three minutes Red Randall and Jimmy Joyce lay motionless listening to the murmuring sounds of the jungle. Birds called and chattered in the distance. A soft wind sighed in the tops of the jungle trees, and there was a peculiar chirping noise from some small animal close by. But they could detect no sounds that would tell them anything about Kagi and his men or the Japs they had obviously failed to ambush.

Suddenly Jimmy Joyce touched Randall and put his lips to his ear.

"You feel it, Red?" he breathed. "I mean, like there is somebody up ahead?"

Randall nodded, for he was experiencing the same sensation. Another scream that died out

142

in a wail came tearing through the jungle. Black man or Jap? Randall could not tell. And when he looked at Jimmy his pal shrugged slightly and gave a puzzled shake of his head. They remained motionless for another few minutes, but there was no other scream. Even the jungle sounds had faded out, and there was a heavy silence that seemed to press them both into the steaming, musty-smelling ground.

"What'll it be, Red?" Jimmy whispered. "Shall we stick here, go ahead and reconnoiter, or what?"

Randall pondered the problem a minute or two. If they remained where they were, the Jap patrol might stumble over them. That would be the end of everything, for, as they had tried to convince Kagi, jungle knives stand little chance against rifles and machine guns. If the Japs did not actually stumble over them, they might find the raft. That would set them to combing the immediate area.

No, it did not seem to be a good idea to stay where they were and do nothing. On the other hand, if they went inland from the stream's bank, they might hopelessly lose themselves. They were in no condition, nor had they the equipment, to battle the jungle for long. If they went ahead, following along the bank of the stream, they might run straight into Jap guns waiting for them.

If the Jap patrol already had wiped out Kagi and his men, Jimmy and he could shove off in the raft and try to find their way to Kagi's brother's village. But, first of all, they must find out what had happened up there ahead. There seemed to be no other choice.

"I vote we reconnoiter up ahead, Jimmy," he finally whispered his decision. "We really can't do anything until we find out what's happened. If the Japs got Kagi's men, and we once get past them, we can make some kind of raft and go on our way down the stream . . . and hope we find that village. What do you think?"

"Decided that was best before I asked you," Jimmy Joyce replied, drawing out the jungle knife he carried under his belt. "Let's go, but stick close, and we'll have to be awfully quiet. Slow and easy is what I say."

"Right. Come on, kiddo," Red Randall breathed.

Red and Jimmy exerted every effort not to so much as snap a vine twig. They made sure of every step before they took it, and all the time they kept darting their eyes every which way for a sign of movement.

Fifteen, twenty torturous minutes dragged by. How far they traveled in that time Red did not know. The important thing was they had not run into danger so far. True, it might be just ahead of them, perhaps lurking behind that next clump of jungle growth.

Randall cut off his rambling thoughts as Jimmy Joyce's fingers curled about his wrist and squeezed tight. He stopped dead in his tracks, and turned his head quickly to look at Jimmy. Joyce was not looking at him. He was peering intently ahead and a little to his left. His hand gripping his jungle knife showed white at the knuckles. Red peered in the direction indicated but saw nothing but a conglomeration of shades of green. Then Jimmy's whisper came to him like the sigh of the wind in the jungle treetops.

"Just beyond those poincianas, Red, I saw something move, and it wasn't a cluster of leaves. Japs in camouflage."

Randall did not turn his head as Jimmy spoke to him. He kept straining his eyes toward the spot. Gradually he made out the figures of two crouching Japs. They wore green-spotted sniper clothes and helmets with netting into which vine leaves had been stuck. They crouched motionless as though dead, and they were facing the other way.

But they were not dead. For in the next instant Randall saw one of them move his small twenty-five caliber machine gun an inch or two. Then the other turned to him and seemed to speak, but Randall could not catch a single sound, though he was only twenty yards away.

Sight of the two Japs made one thing certain to Randall. Kagi's surprise attack had failed to wipe out the Jap patrol. On the other hand, the two Japs were evidence that neither had Kagi and all his men been wiped out. It seemed quite probable that some of them had melted into the jungle and the Japs were striving to track them down.

To Red Randall and Jimmy Joyce, those two crouching Japs were a barrier. They could not go forward and they could not return to the raft, for now the raft would be the most dangerous spot of all.

Randall took his eyes off the Japs and looked steadily at Jimmy. Young Joyce returned his stare with one that was equally steady, and nodded his head. Red grinned tightly and moved until his lips were a fraction of an inch from Jimmy's ear.

"They've got to be ours, or else!" he breathed. "We can't wait for them to go away. Ease a little to your left, and I'll ease a bit to my right. That way we'll come in on them from different angles. Take it slow, and we must keep each other in sight. If we lose contact we'll be sunk sure. All set?"

Jimmy nodded, and they started wiggling off in opposite directions.

For several yards as Randall snaked forward, he kept one eye on the Japs and one eye on Jimmy Joyce off to his left. Then the dense jungle growth took a hand and completely hid Jimmy from him. He could not see so much as a leaf move to indicate where Jimmy was. Anger and fear battled in his heart, but neither caused him to pause in his progress. He crawled onward until only five yards of jungle separated him from the Japs.

And that was the moment for which the gods of mocking fate had been waiting!

Randall took his eyes off the Japs, and turned his head to the left to see if he could spot Jimmy. For the attack to be successful they must make it together. But he saw no sign of Jimmy Joyce. When he looked toward the Japs again, both of them made queer soft sounds in their throats and dived straight forward and disappeared as though they had shot themselves through an open door and slammed it shut.

Red froze as the rage of defeat surged through him, and then he dropped flat when a wild scream tore through the jungle. He could not tell from whence the scream had come, or whether or not it had come from a human throat. Had the Japs been aware of his coming and dived into the thick jungle to circle about and trap him? Had they seen something else? Could it have been Kagi, or one of his men? What was the meaning of the scream? What of Jimmy Joyce? It was all he could do to refrain from making some sound that Jimmy would hear and understand and repeat to assure him that he was all right. But he knew that any sound he made now would be his undoing.

Instinct told Red Randall that there was a Jap lurking near by. The steaming heat of the jungle pressed against him like a soggy blanket. His temples throbbed, and he hardly dared breathe for fear that the Jap would hear him. He could not see the Nip, nor could he hear him. But he felt sure that he was somewhere just in front of him, perhaps hugging the ground behind that next clump of jungle growth, or perched in the branches of a tree.

Suddenly he saw shadowy movement in front of him. His fingers tightened on the bone handle of his jungle knife as he made out the telltale blurred green uniform of a Jap. Savage determination gripped him. The Jap had made the first move; that was fine!

"You'll never see Tokyo again, you Jap rat!" Randall thought as he hurled himself at the shadowy movement just in front of him.

What happened in the next split second or two was like a series of pictures, each one flashing across the screen of Randall's eyes to be gone in a twinkling. He saw the shadow twist around. He saw a helmeted head jerk back. He saw double-lidded eyes go wide and gleaming. He saw twin rows of buckteeth as lips parted to cry out. And lastly he saw the Jap fold up and crumple to the ground.

Randall did not pause to gloat over his victory. He snatched up the light machine gun from the

Jap's limp fingers and threw himself to one side. Up he came on his knees, finger crooked about the trigger, and eyes darting about in all directions.

It was Red's good fortune that he possessed a sense of instinctive self-preservation. Hardly had he come up on his knees than he found himself staring past a jungle bush at a little clearing. Into the clearing rushed four Jap soldiers. They seemed to be charging straight toward him, but Randall did not stop to figure whether or not that was the case. Sight and action were one for him. He brought up the Jap machine gun, sighted quickly, and pulled the trigger. The gun made a peculiar soft popping sound, but there was nothing soft about its bullets. They ripped into one Jap, and then the next, and the next, and the next, until all four had stumbled and fallen to the ground.

"Five from eight leaves three!" Randall muttered as he darted his eyes to the left and right. "So . . ."

He stopped as two more figures came leaping out of nowhere into the clearing. But they were not Japs. They were Kagi and one of his warriors.

"Down, Kagi, you fool!" Red barked.

The tribe chieftain stopped short. His eyes darted Randall's way, and went as big as dinner plates when he saw him.

"You make bang, bang?" he boomed out in a stunned voice. "Kagi no good. You big fight man. All Japs die. Kagi kill so many."

The native chief held up three fingers, and then patted the jungle knife he held in his huge hand. Randall was elated. He stepped over the dead Jap and out into the clearing. And then the greatest relief and joy, too, was his. Jimmy Joyce came leaping out into the clearing from off to the left.

"Fine guy, a fine guy!" Jimmy cried happily as he raced over. "I don't even get the chance for a hit, and you up and clear the bases. I ask you, is that nice?"

"No, not a bit nice," Red replied as he looked down at the bullet-riddled Japs. "But don't ever tell anybody because nobody would believe that one guy could have so much luck. One simply made a bad pass and I got him. The others just walked into this gun I'd snitched from the first one. I was plenty scared, and plenty worried over what had happened to you, Jimmy."

Young Joyce flushed and smiled thinly.

"And don't you ever tell anybody about *me* in this thing," he said. "I went head over heels into a mud hole, and had one heck of a job trying to get out. Take a look at me, if you don't believe it."

Jimmy looked as well as smelled his experience. "We'll dunk you in the stream and wring you out," Red said with a chuckle. Then as he felt Kagi's black eyes fixed on him, he turned his head to the native. "Where other men?" he asked. "Japs make die?"

The chief hung his head like a whipped dog. He held up two fingers.

"Japs make die so many," he said in a heavy voice. "Kagi no good. White friend much good. Kagi no listen to talk when white friends make talk. Kagi bad chief. You good chief. You talk Kagi. Kagi do."

Randall started to laugh, but checked himself. Somehow he felt that this moment was some kind of crisis in the life of the native. His surprise attack had failed. He had lost two of his men, and perhaps humiliated himself in the eyes of the others. To be laughed at by white men, even in a kindly way, might be too much for him. Red knew little about the handling of Southwest Pacific natives, but he possessed cold, hard common sense, and he put it to full use now. He shook his head at the native chief.

"No, Kagi," he said quietly. "Kagi good. Kagi's men good, too. Jap guns bad. Japs have big ears. Hear much. Learn to hear in jungle. Japs make war longa time. Learn much. Kagi no understand that. Kagi brave. Much brave. Kagi kill three Japs. That good. White friends glad. Where Kagi's men?"

The chief's head came up, and his eyes and ebony face were aglow with pride. He reached out a long arm and touched Randall on the shoulder.

"White friend good friend," he said solemnly. "No forget. Kagi no let white friend die. Maybe Kagi die. White friend no die. Kagi's men wait raft now."

"Then we go," Randall nodded and pointed in the direction of the raft. "Maybe much more Japs near. Hear bang, bang. We go quick. Go your brother's village."

Kagi nodded and pointed toward the west.

"Brother's village close," he said. "Sun low we see brother's village. We go. Kagi glad. All Japs die."

"If only *all* of them *were* dead!" Randall muttered and turned to follow Kagi out of the clearing.

✥ *Chapter XIII* ✥

"WILD WILLIE"
WILKINS

WHEN RED RANDALL was five years old his father had taken him to see his first movie. In breathless excitement he had sat in his seat and stared at the blank screen. And then suddenly it was not blank any more. Instead there were trees, and flowers, and hills, and houses, and people. He had been completely awed.

Right now he was experiencing a little of the emotion that had been his then. After traveling down a seemingly endless stream, with nothing but jungle growth on each bank, they suddenly came to a huge native village of kunai grass and split bamboo huts. It was like magic that it should appear so suddenly, and for a moment, until Kagi loudly hailed one of half a dozen natives moving about, he thought his eyes were playing him tricks.

The natives spun about at the sound of Kagi's booming voice, and rushed down to the edge of the stream. Kagi muttered to his men and they turned the raft and poled it toward the shore. It was then that Randall noticed that the stream had widened out considerably at this point. Further ahead it emptied into the Pacific.

No sooner had the raft been grounded than Kagi leaped ashore and immediately engaged in excited talk with the others. By the time Red Randall and Jimmy Joyce, breathing silent prayers of thanks and relief, stepped ashore, Kagi was scowling and shaking his head in puzzled anger.

"What's wrong, Kagi?" Randall asked. "Your brother no live here no more?"

"Him say my brother and men go with white friend soldiers to kill Japs," Kagi replied, pointing to one of the natives. "Go longa, longa time.

Many suns, him say. Him say white boss man stay my brother's village. Him take us to white boss man."

"Then let's go," Red and Jimmy said simultaneously. "Maybe white boss man tell us all about your brother."

Kagi turned to those who had met the raft. Before he could say anything, one of the natives shouted in his own tongue and all the others turned to look back at the village. A shaggy-haired, bearded man, wearing a sun-bleached, tattered field uniform of an Australian major, came striding toward the bank. With him were two junior officers, one of whom wore a Yank uniform. Behind them, like a rear guard, trailed four natives.

The bearded major reached the waiting group and started to bark at Kagi in his native tongue. As his deep brown eyes caught sight of Red, he stopped in amazement.

"You're white?" he demanded. "Is that a Yank flier's uniform you're wearing?"

"Yes, sir," Red replied with a grin. "Captain Randall, attached to Major Pratt's fighters at Seven Mile Field, Port Moresby. This is Captain Joyce from the same field, sir."

"Pratt, eh?" the other echoed in a glad tone. "Still at Moresby? Good! Been worried that maybe the blasted Nips had taken Moresby, too. I know Pratt well. Good man in any kind of show."

The Australian abruptly turned to Kagi and started talking to him in his native tongue. When he had finished, Kagi beamed at Randall and Joyce, then with the others walked away.

"I'm Major Wilkins, Captains," the Australian said, again turning his attention to the young airmen. "This is Lieutenant Berry of your own country. And this is Lieutenant Lismore of my old regiment. Come along all of you to my diggings."

Randall shook hands with the two lieutenants and mumbled automatic greetings. They were automatic for the reason that his thoughts were spinning. He suddenly remembered hearing things, reading things, and seeing pictures of the famed Major "Wild Willie" Wilkins. Because of his daring exploits in and about Jap-held territory, the man had been dubbed the Australian Lawrence of Arabia. There was not a soldier in the Southwest Pacific battle area who had not heard of "Wild Willie" Wilkins. "Wild Willie" and his men had been doing in the Solomons and New Guinea what Wingate and his Raiders had been doing in Burma. To meet the man under these circumstances almost took Randall's breath away, and in somewhat of a daze he walked with the others to a large kunai grass hut which served as Wilkins' quarters.

"Sit down, gentlemen," the man said, waving a hand at several native-built chairs. "We don't stand on ceremony here. Want something to eat, and some coconut milk?"

In their excitement neither Randall nor Joyce was hungry enough or thirsty enough to bother. They shook their heads.

"No thanks, sir," Red declined for them both.

"Moresby, eh?" the senior officer mused with a sort of sigh in his voice. "How long ago were you there? Shot down, eh, and found by Kagi? How is Moresby making out? Are we going to be able to hold off the enemy, the filthy devils?"

Randall had to think for a moment before he could reply. It seemed a year since he had taken off from Seven Mile Field.

"Five days, sir," he answered the Major's first question. "We're holding at Port Moresby and will get stronger. The Japs are trying to get over the Owen Stanleys from Buna way. There is a large force reported ashore down at Milne Bay. It was at Milne Bay where Joyce and I had our tough luck. A case of too many Zeros. Some of Kagi's men found me, and Kagi and some of the others found Joyce. The luckiest break we ever had."

"So Moresby's still there, eh?" Wilkins grunted and smiled with pleasure. "Makes me feel a hundred per cent better. I left Moresby four months ago. Been here ever since. Like a blasted animal with both feet caught fast in a trap. A force down

Milne Bay way, eh? We figured something like that. Figured they were feeding their planes through to Milne Bay. Well, we hope to put a stop to that."

The Major fell silent and stared down at his clenched fists. "Pardon me, Major," Randall said, "but Kagi said his brother, the chief of this village, told him that a boatload of troops came ashore here under Jap fire after their boat was sunk. Is that true, sir? Is that how you got here? I didn't know there were any Australians or Americans on New Guinea outside of the Port Moresby area."

"That's how we got here, fortunately or unfortunately, according to how you look at it," "Wild Willie" Wilkins replied. Then with a grimace, he said, "The results of one of my little stunts that backfired. There were two hundred of us aboard a small lugger. We were trying to sneak around under the cover of night, holing up in some stream mouth by day, to get in back of the Nips at Buna and raise merry Ned with their supply bases. Well, one nightfall a couple of Jap bombers spotted us sneaking out. We started out too early, I readily confess. The bombers missed us by a mile, though we all got a good ducking. When the Nips went away we tried it again, fools that we were to try it again so soon!"

The Major paused and his deep brown eyes flashed fire as a wave of bitterness and anger went through him.

"A Jap submarine caught us just offshore," he continued presently. "Threw shells and torpedoes, everything they had aboard, I guess. It wasn't nice. Our lugger started down fast. One of those short but mighty tough storms out this way came up, and that didn't help either. We launched what boats we could, and tossed all the rafts over. We were still trying to make shore at dawn when some Nip bombers came along. They bombed and strafed us pretty bad. A hundred and fifty of us finally made the shore, but fifteen were badly wounded. They died that same day. We had salvaged everything we could, and we were able to get away with quite a bit of equipment. But we were a sorry-looking lot, and pretty much done in. Then Laloki, that's Kagi's brother, and some of his men showed up and things began to get better. Laloki had helped me before; we're old friends."

The Major paused again and smiled faintly.

"If we pull off our little show successfully," he went on in a moment or two, "the credit will belong to Laloki. He is the one who told us about the place. He and his men have been helping us ambush Nip patrols; we take their guns to replace those we lost with the lugger. Yes, we have Laloki and his men to thank for a chance to give the Jap a hard blow."

Randall leaned forward as tingling excitement stepped up his heart beat.

"I'm afraid I don't quite follow you, sir," he said. "Just what is the little show that you expect to pull off?"

"Wild Willie" Wilkins looked at him with mild amusement. "Sorry, Captain," he said. "So used to talking it over with my officers and men, I completely lost sight of the fact that you wouldn't know anything about it. Well, we've located a secret airfield of the Nips on this end of New Guinea. They've practically cut it out of the heart of the jungle with their bare hands. It's about seventy miles from here, west by southwest. I doubt that it can be seen from the air, though I haven't flown over the place. From the ground you're almost on it before you realize it. I imagine that they plan to use it as a bomber and fighter base for their drive on Moresby. Right now, it's a feeder base, you might say, a stopping place for aircraft coming over from New Britain. I believe, too, that it's a plane depot for aircraft flown in off their carriers. The last time I visited the spot, which was just four days ago, they had about five hundred aircraft of all types based there."

Red and Jimmy whistled softly. The Major nodded as though to confirm his words.

"At least five hundred aircraft," he reiterated, "and more equipment than you could shake a stick at. Must have brought it overland on their shoulders. We'll have a scrap on our hands, but we'll take that place away from them, no fear. If we can't take it, we'll reduce it to a mosquito roost."

"With only a hundred and thirty-five men, sir?" Jimmy gasped.

"Plus Laloki, and a good hundred of his men," the Major replied with a nod. "We've had to wait to do this job because we've had to spend a lot of time ambushing odd Jap patrols to pick up enough arms and ammunition to outfit Laloki's men. A couple of months ago we had hopes of getting supplies and some help. We sent a runner to Moresby asking for someone to fly down here to get the picture. He got through because a pilot came and landed down the shore a way. Lieutenant Berry contacted him and told him what he wanted. The pilot took off but no sooner did he get into the air than four Zeros piled down on him. The last we saw of him he was streaking down the shore line trying to shake them off. That was about a month ago. I guess he didn't get through. We haven't heard a word from Moresby since. We haven't any radio, of course. But no help came, so I was beginning to give up hope that Moresby was still in our hands."

"Stone, that was Stone!" Randall cried and looked at Jimmy Joyce. Then turning back to Major Wilkins, he said, "That pilot did get through to Port Moresby, sir, just before Joyce and I took off for the Milne Bay raid. He crash-landed, though, and was killed. There was enough evidence to show that he had been captured by the Japs and tortured. They must have forced him down on some stretch of beach and taken him prisoner. Somehow he managed to escape and actually got away in his own plane. The poor fellow! He came so darn close to success."

"There's one point that doesn't check with what we learned at Seven Mile from Major Pratt, sir," Jimmy Joyce spoke up. "That runner you sent said only that there was a wounded officer in a native village at Baniara. He said the officer was an American and was dying and wanted an Intelli-

gence officer to be sent to him. Stone was sent because he had been connected with Intelligence
at one time. Didn't the native runner return to
this village?"

"We never saw him again," the Major said with
a shake of his head. "The Nips probably caught
him on the way back. But the poor fellow got the
message we gave him all mixed up. It was Lieutenant Berry, sitting right there beside you, who
sent him. He was wounded, but he wasn't that
bad."

"No more than a scratch," Berry spoke up with
a grin. "I gave the native the message verbally,
as well as wrote it down. I learned from Stone that
the native had lost the written message, and that
all he could remember was that I was wounded,
badly so he thought, and wanted to contact another Intelligence officer. He didn't say a thing
about the others down here, so Stone was stunned
when he found out what the picture really was.
Poor Stone! What a rotten way for it all to end
for him."

Jimmy Joyce nodded in silent sympathy, and for a moment no one spoke. Each no doubt was thinking of how many little twists of fate had made things what they were. If the runner had not lost the written message, High Command at Port Moresby would have learned what had happened to Wilkins' raiding party, where they were, and what they needed. If Stone had not been captured, he could have taken back the whole story and lived. And supplies and air assistance that Wilkins badly needed would be his right now.

"You're going through with it, sir?" Randall murmured. "I mean you aren't going to wait and try to get the whole truth through to Moresby?"

"No, I'm not going to wait," the Major said with a grim set of his chin. "I can't. My troops are in position now. If one of you had brought a plane along, I'd send you to Moresby with a demand for more supplies and air help, and put off the attack for a few days. But you arrived by raft, and so I head into the jungle first thing come dawn. In three days I'll be with my troops who are in hiding and waiting for me. On the next day we'll hit the Japs. They'll outnumber us three to one in men and in guns. If some of their planes get into the air, that will make it tougher for us. All we have in our favor is surprise . . . and fighting guts."

The steel-hard look in the Major's eyes reflected the fighting qualities of this great leader of the daring band of raiders. On impulse Red glanced at Joyce, caught the look in Jimmy's eyes, and turned back to "Wild Willie" Wilkins.

"We didn't arrive with our planes, unfortunately, sir," he said quietly. "But we did bring along the ability to shoot a machine gun or rifle and use a jungle knife. If you have places for us in your plans, sir, we'd like nothing better than to be included in the party."

"Your request was unnecessary, Captain," the other said with a grin. "I had already included you. Two extra men who can shoot is two more than I had hoped for. Might even swing the balance in our favor, you never can tell. That's settled then. Now you need food and as much rest as you can get. We start at dawn on a seventy-mile trek through the jungle. That won't be any stroll about the park. You'll need every ounce of strength you can store up. Thanks for joining up with us. You won't find it boring."

The Major's last words left an ominous ring in Randall s ears!

Chapter XIV

A DARING PLAN

RED RANDALL wiped rivulets of sweat from his face, brushed aside the cloud of winged insects that milled about just over his head, and shifted the straps of the pack on his back. He was squatting on the ground.

"Boy, I've only got one wish in life now!" he said to Jimmy Joyce squatting beside him. "That's to grow up to be a grandfather."

"I'd like to live to a ripe old age myself," Jimmy said, "but why the grandfather part?"

"So I could see the expressions on the faces of my grandchildren when I tell them how their grandpop traveled seventy miles through New Guinea jungle in three days. And I do mean jungle!"

Jimmy laughed. "They'll look at you in wonder, and think what a cockeyed liar old grandpa is getting to be!"

"They probably will," Red grinned. "To tell you the truth, I was thinking the same thing about the Major when he told us back at Baniara that he was coming this far in three days. And speaking of the Major, when is he coming back, I wonder?"

"When he gets ready," Jimmy grunted. "He knows his onions, so don't worry about him."

"Who's worrying?" Red asked. "I'm only anxious to get a look at that Jap secret field he said he'd show us as soon as he had checked with his various units. Sure is hard to believe that there's an air strip within a thousand miles of this mess of jungle."

Randall gazed about the small clearing. Jungle, nothing but jungle everywhere, on all sides, and a canopy above that blotted out the sun. A few yards away from him some twenty dark-skinned natives sat hunched motionless beside packs big enough and heavy enough for a mule to carry.

Kagi was among them, and his great size made him stand out like a mountain among hills.

Red looked toward him and grinned. Kagi caught his eye and grinned back. A warm feeling toward the big fellow surged through Randall. Since the very start of this jungle trip Kagi had been practically a shadow for Jimmy and himself. He had performed a thousand and one little services for them without which they would have suffered far more than they had. It was Kagi's way of showing his respect and admiration for what Randall had done to that Jap patrol.

At first Randall had been uneasy and afraid that "Wild Willie" Wilkins might not approve such display of favoritism. On this trip it had been really a case of every man for himself and stragglers strictly out of luck. But the Major had given no indication of annoyance and so Randall had willingly accepted Kagi's help. The truth of the matter was that Kagi had told his brother's men of Randall's deed, and in time the story of that little battle had reached Major Wilkins' ears. The

Major knew well the ways of the black man, and the workings of his childish mind. To refuse Kagi the right to serve the two Yank pilots, who he regarded almost as his masters, could lead to serious trouble among the natives. So "Wild Willie" Wilkins had said nothing. The big task had been to make all speed through the jungle to where his troops awaited him.

That journey was now a thing of the past. Last night the party had camped for the last time. Just two hours ago Wilkins had contacted the first unit of his waiting men. Leaving Red and Jimmy to wait with Kagi and the others, Wilkins had gone on a quick inspection tour with his two aides, Lieutenants Berry and Lismore.

At first Red had been a little disappointed that the Major had not taken him along. But he was glad now, and he had a hunch that Wilkins had noticed how truly exhausted he was and had left Jimmy and him behind to rest.

Randall's thoughts were interrupted when the jungle growth before him parted like a green curtain and Major Wilkins stepped into view. Directly behind him was a giant native who carried a machine gun in one hand with all the ease a grown man would carry a boy's water pistol. Randall heard Kagi grunt behind him, and then Kagi swept past, ignoring Wilkins, and broke into breathless jabber with the other native.

"The brothers meet," Major Wilkins said as he came over to Red and Jimmy, who had hastily gotten to their feet. "That's Laloki, Kagi's brother. Dump your packs, but keep your machine guns. They'll take care of the other stuff. You two can stick with me. I think that would be best in view of the fact that you're not experienced in this kind of fighting. Besides, I've got everything worked out as I want it to go. Every man knows exactly what he must do. So you stick with me, and follow my lead. Right now I'll give you a look at our objective. Shed your packs and follow me. Walk softly, though, and no talking."

Red and Jimmy hastily shed their packs from

their backs, picked up the machine gun that Wilkins had given to each of them, and followed the famous raider out of the small jungle clearing. As they walked by Kagi and Laloki, the latter fixed wide eyes on Red and Jimmy, and his crooked white teeth flashed in a smile.

For a good half-hour they followed silently in Major Wilkins' footsteps. More than once Red had the uneasy feeling that Jap eyes were watching his every move, and that snipers' sights were fixed squarely upon him. Several times he wanted to ask the Major to slow up the pace, but each time he checked his impulse. He had asked for a chance to serve under the famous raider, and he would rather drop dead in his tracks than admit that he had not the strength to keep up. Deep down he had the feeling that Jimmy and he were about to take part in a history-making episode—certainly one which, if successful, would go far toward turning the tide in favor of General MacArthur's forces. To capture and completely destroy a Jap air base so strategically located would indeed be a serious blow to the enemy and his plans for total occupation of New Guinea.

Could Major Wilkins succeed in this bold venture with two hundred and fifty men, only half of whom were trained soldiers? "Wild Willie" Wilkins was going to tackle the gigantic task, and as long as there was a drop of fighting blood in his body, he would keep on banging away at the doors that barred him from his goal.

Abruptly Major Wilkins came to a halt and dropped silently to the ground. He turned his head and silently motioned for Randall and Joyce to creep up on either side of him. When they were close beside him, the Major reached out with one hand to part a curtain of vines, and pointed ahead and a little down with his other hand.

"There it is," he whispered. "Clever devils the Japs, aren't they?"

Randall found that he was on the crest of a two or three-hundred-foot hill that sloped away in front of him for a distance of perhaps half a mile.

At the end of the slope, a strip of solid green, about sixty yards wide, extended for a good third of a mile. At first glance it seemed as though he was looking down on jungle so thick and close-grown that it looked like solid ground. From the air he knew that it would blend in so perfectly with the surrounding area that it would not stand out at all.

"That's an air strip, sir?" he heard his own whispering voice ask incredulously.

"That's just what it is," came the reply. "And just about the finest job of camouflaging I've ever seen. They leveled it flat but left clipped-off stubble so that planes taking off would raise no clouds of dust. As I told you, Laloki practically walked onto it before he realized what it was. It was his good fortune that no Jap saw him before he ducked back into the jungle and made tracks back to his village. Here, take my glasses and pay particular attention to what's under the trees that flank both sides."

Randall accepted the binoculars the Major

handed him, put them to his eyes, and adjusted them to the distance. The strip of solid green seemed to leap right up to the end of his nose. It was still just a solid strip of green, but on either side, and drawn well back under the overhanging branches of the trees, were Jap planes of all sizes and types, wing tip to wing tip. He made out Zeros, Mitsubishis, and Nakajimas. There were double rows of planes, and although it was impossible to count them individually, he was certain that there were between four and five hundred parked there.

He could see not only the planes, but also men wandering about under the trees, or swarming over the parked aircraft. Blurred silverish movement told him that even as he watched some of the engines were being warmed up. He gaped wide-eyed, until Jimmy Joyce reached across Major Wilkins' back and gently but firmly lifted the binoculars out of his hands. He let them go without protest, and turned to stare into the

Major's bearded face. The famous raider grinned tight-lipped and arched one eyebrow.

"Quite a prize, eh?" he murmured.

Randall had to swallow before he spoke. That some two hundred and fifty men could capture and destroy the airdrome seemed utterly fantastic. With all those planes, there must be hundreds of Japs to guard them, take care of them, and fly them. It would take half a division, not two hundred and fifty men to capture that Jap air base.

"I—I don't know what to say, sir!" Red finally breathed.

"Don't bother, for I know what you're thinking," the Major said and broadened his smile. "But the job often isn't as big or as impossible as it looks. The main thing is to find the weak spots, and concentrate our attack on those points. But we've got to possess the advantage of surprise to stand even a fighting chance. When the attack begins, one unit will go for their radio station and capture it intact. That will cut short their chances to whistle up help. Another unit will charge the commander's headquarters and grab him and his staff. Take his officers away and the Jap runs in circles. Another unit will go for the fuel dump and blow it sky high.

"We've spent two months studying that spot, and we know it as well as though we'd built it ourselves. We'll strike at dawn tomorrow. The Jap is not on his toes then. We need not worry about other planes coming in, for they land or take-off just before sundown. Oh, we've got everything worked out, never fear. But there is one little item that bothers me."

A sudden hunch was Red Randall's, but he decided not to mention it. In the Major's eyes it might seem silly.

"What is that something, sir?" he asked instead.

"Wild Willie" Wilkins scowled and nodded toward the solid green air strip.

"The pilots and those planes," he said. "If we let them get any planes into the air, it isn't going to be good at all. A couple of those Zeros strafing us will put us in bad shape in no time. The natives are fine for ground hand-to-hand fighting, but let Jap planes come down on them and they take to the jungle. That's my only real worry—that we won't click fast enough to stop them from getting any planes off."

Jimmy Joyce had had his look at the camouflaged air strip through the binoculars and was looking across Wilkins' back at Red with a peculiar gleam in his eye. Red caught the look and half nodded.

"Have you any special plan of attack to handle that possibility, sir?" he addressed himself to the Major.

"None but to surprise the pants off them," the senior officer said, "and gain a commanding position so that we can blast any pilot who tries to take off."

Randall grunted absently and turned his head to stare at the air strip for a moment. A commanding position, eh? There would have to be more than one commanding position gained on that strip to prevent aircraft from taking off. He knew from experience that a Zero did not require half the distance allowed by the strip, so it followed that Wilkins' men would have to be stationed all along both sides of the strip to prevent any take-offs. And the famous raider did not have nearly enough men.

"Mind if I say something, sir, as . . . well as a sort of outsider?" he asked quietly.

Wilkins gave him a keen stare and shook his head.

"Not at all," he said. "Go ahead."

"You haven't got enough men, sir, to stop every Jap from taking off," Randall said bluntly. "You'd have to cover every inch of the strip, and even then you couldn't be sure. Zeros can take off in a very short distance. A couple of them would be bound to get into the air. I'd bet anything on it. However . . ."

Randall sort of stumbled on the rest and

stopped talking as he felt his face glow under the Major's steady stare.

"Go on," Wilkins ordered. "However, what? You seem to have something important on your mind. What is it?"

Red glanced at Jimmy for moral support but Jimmy had the binoculars to his eyes again and was focusing them on the air strip.

"Perhaps Joyce and I could prevent that, sir," he said slowly, looking straight into the other's eyes. "I mean, of course, sir, unless it would upset your general plan of action."

"I don't know *what* you mean, yet!" the Major said evenly. "Get it out and let's have a look at it."

"I mean that with some covering support, Joyce and I could rush a couple of those Zeros and get them into the air," Red practically blurted out. "Once we're in the air we'd see to it that nobody else came up aloft. We've both flown the Zero and can operate its guns. But I don't mean to infer, sir, that . . ."

"Never mind that, I understand," the Major cut in sharply. "I'll make any change in my plans if it will help the outcome. Now, what do you mean by some covering support?"

Red thought that question over a moment before he answered.

"For one thing, sir," he finally said, "some of your men, say half a dozen, to help Joyce and me charge a couple of the Zeros, and keep the Japs off our necks until we can get in and take off. We might be lucky enough to grab two with props ticking over, but we don't want to bank on it. If we've got to boot the engines into life, it's going to take a minute or two longer. And that's a long time if no one else is around to keep the Japs too busy to take pot shots at us.

"Also, a divertive action a distance away from the planes we pick would be helpful. You'll have to inform your native troops that the two Zeros that will take-off will be piloted by friends, so they'll not break and hit for the jungle if we should start to do a little strafing on our own. Once Joyce and I are in the air, I promise you that we'll handle any other planes that try to take off."

As Randall finished speaking, half expecting a snort to come from the other's lips, "Wild Willie" Wilkins stared at him harder than ever. Then suddenly the bearded warrior chuckled softly.

"Some people would call that reckless boasting, Randall," he said. "But I don't. I like a man to have complete faith in his ability to do something. I like your suggestion so much that I'm going to accept it without any argument. Your pilot touch to this thing is exactly what it needs. It makes me feel surer of victory just to hear you mention it. However, determination to do something, and accomplishing same, are two things that can be far removed from each other. I'll give you the six men you need, six of my best who can fan the buckteeth out of a Jap's mouth at two hundred yards. You may bump into only a couple of Jap mechanics, and you may bump into two hundred of them armed to the teeth; remember that. There's no guarantee that it won't get too hot and cost you both your lives."

Major Wilkins stopped and seemed to wait for Randall to say something. And Randall did not keep him waiting.

"Neither Joyce nor I came along for the walk, sir," he said evenly. "If we fail and stop a couple, why . . . why, that will be our tough luck."

"Wild Willie" Wilkins liked that reply. His grin and the look in his eyes showed plainly that he liked it.

"A deal, and thank you both," he said. Then reaching over and taking the binoculars from Jimmy Joyce, he added, "Time we got back. I've got to shift plans about a bit, pick your six cover men, and spread the word that the two Zeros will not be piloted by . . ."

The Major bit off the last and spun around. So did Red and Jimmy. Crouched on the ground not five feet from them was Kagi. He blinked, and parted his lips in the flash of a smile.

"Kagi hear talk," he said solemnly, bobbing his head up and down. "Where white man-bird friends go, Kagi go."

Chapter XV

WINGS OF VENGEANCE

THE FIRST sign of dawn was a pale wave of light that stole timidly up over the eastern lip of the world, and seemed to hesitate and tremble when it met the blackness of night. In another few moments it would come with a mighty rush and another night would scurry off in hasty retreat. Right now, though, night was still king, and the New Guinea jungle was deathly still as though in fearful obedience of a royal command.

Crouched motionless on the ground at a point not over one hundred and fifty yards from one end of the camouflaged Jap air strip, Red Randall stared at the pale light in the east and wondered what tricks of fortune the fates would play on

"Wild Willie" Wilkins' raiders by the time the new sun had climbed to the zenith and descended below the western edge of the world. No tingling fears rippled through him, and he was more than a little surprised that he felt so calm and unmoved. The explanation for that might be because everything seemed so unreal to him. He was used to war in the air. Up there it was clean and fresh, and you could see your foe, and it was either he or you. Down here in the jungle it was entirely different. When you saw your foe at all, it was only as swift movement in the tangled green mass of jungle.

He turned his head and stared at the seven motionless shadows of men that hugged the ground with him. Right next to him was Jimmy Joyce, and for all he could tell Jimmy might be snatching a last few winks of sleep. But he knew that was not true. He was quite sure that Jimmy's mind was filled with rambling thoughts, too. Beyond Jimmy were the six raiders whom Major Wilkins had selected to hold off any Japs while

Jimmy and he got a couple of Zeros into the air. Three were Yanks and three were Australians, six of the toughest soldiers Red ever hoped to have the pleasure of meeting. For the life of him, as he stared at their motionless forms now, he could not think of a single one of their names, though but a bare two hours ago he was sure that he knew them all by heart.

Why had he forgotten their names? He wondered about that. Was it because death was to be their lot, and it would be best for him to remember them as a fighting unit that had made Jimmy's and his success possible, and not as individual men with names? Was there some invisible force or power that made you forget names so that the pain of loss through death would be less personal?

He dismissed the thought and turned his head to the other side. A faint smile tugged at the corners of his mouth when he made out the outlines of huge Kagi—Kagi the good servant now, the great faithful Saint Bernard, who would undoubtedly have started a one-man war if Major

Wilkins had not permitted him to accompany Red and Jimmy on this special mission.

A word from the sergeant in charge of the raiders sent Randall's eyes flying to the dial of his wrist watch. He slipped off the cover to reveal the radium painted figures, and saw that it lacked but two minutes before H-hour.

No shot would signal the beginning of the attack on the Jap air strip. Major Wilkins had posted his attacking units in the jungle all about the air strip, and it would be impossible for a shot to be heard by all. Also, each unit had some one hundred and fifty yards to travel before actual contact with the enemy would be made. Therefore all watches had been synchronized, and when the hands reached a specified point, movement forward would begin. All units should make contact with the enemy at practically the same time, and it was hoped that the element of surprise would throw the enemy into turmoil.

Two minutes to go. One minute. Fifty seconds . . . forty seconds . . . thirty . . .

A hand gripped Randall's shoulder, and Jimmy whispered in his ears. "Luck, Red. Get your baby up, and fly like nobody's business!"

Red grinned and squeezed Joyce's hand on his arm. "And how, boy!" he breathed. "Be sure you come up with me, kiddo. Can't do it alone. It'll take the two of us."

Fifteen seconds! At that instant the brooding silence ahead was shattered by aircraft engines barking into life. Randall saw the momentary purple flash of exhaust plumes, which came from the near end of the air strip. Were they testing engines after a night of jungle damp? Or were the Nips going to confound "Wild Willie" Wilkins' painstaking observations and do some flying so early in the morning?

Three seconds . . . two seconds . . . one. Randall's thoughts fled as he came up onto his feet. The others rose with him, and with the sergeant in the lead they dropped into single file and started moving silently forward. The machine gun that Randall carried, with his finger curled about the trigger, felt good and comforting in his hands, and grim determination and confidence were like cooling waters flowing over his hot and sticky body.

Randall took a brief second to glance down at his watch as he slipped the dial cover off. Five more minutes and they would be at the near edge of the air strip and racing into gun-spitting action. It was still dark and he hoped that "Wild Willie" Wilkins was sure of the time element. The gray light of dawn would help them, but the darkness of night might result in chaos.

Now the five minutes were spent. The jungle ended and the cropped ground of the air strip was actually under his feet. Once out of the jungle, pale light flooded everything. The sound of idling aircraft engines was off to his left. Machine-gun fire broke out like rolling thunder, punctuated by the sharper, clearer blasts of exploding hand grenades.

Red Randall spun around to his left and charged forward, his machine gun held in front of him.

Beside him was Kagi, whose mighty war yells could be heard above the chattering and yammering all about. With one hand he fired his machine gun, while he waved his jungle knife in his other hand high above his head.

It was not until Randall had taken a dozen racing steps that he clearly saw what was in front of them. Planes, planes, and more planes. And Japs, twenty or thirty of them, naked to the waist and standing rooted in their tracks, stunned by this sudden onslaught beyond all power of movement. Red saw at least half a dozen fall silently to the ground like felled trees as machine-gun bullets reached them. He saw two planes burst into flame, and columns of orange-tinted smoke spew up through the jungle tree branches. A weird light instantly flowed over everything.

The paralysis that had pinned the Japs helpless suddenly left them and they became a bunch of screaming maniacs. Some dived for guns they had left near by, but most of them died before their hands touched metal. Others ran in circles, or collided with wing tips to go sprawling on the ground. A few streaked off into the jungle screaming like mortally wounded jackals.

The flames from two planes whose gas tanks obviously had been hit spread to the planes on either side of them, and a terrible fear gripped Randall that before the others and he could drive the Japs clear, the whole place would become a gigantic roaring inferno of flame. That fear quickly vanished, for then it seemed as though Lady Luck tapped him on the shoulder, pointed, and said, "Look at those first two Zeros with props ticking over! Do you want me to do more?"

Jimmy Joyce saw the two Zeros at practically the same instant. Oddly enough a Jap was crouched under each plane, like a cornered dog, though each clutched a gun in his hands. A gun chattered inches from Randall's right ear. One Jap dropped his gun and melted into the ground. Then something black zoomed by Randall. It was

Kagi. His knife flashed in the weird light, and the Jap crouching under the other plane was no longer a menace.

Randall tossed his machine gun to Kagi, then dived into the cockpit of the Zero nearest him. Hardly had he hit the seat than a swarm of angry metal hornets whined over his head. He ducked instinctively, kicked off the Zero's brakes and reached for the throttle. The engine in the nose roared and the plane moved forward.

Out of the corner of his eye he saw three Japs racing toward him. They flung up their rifles, but faithful Kagi was on the job. The big chief seemed to rise up out of the ground in front of the running Japs. Randall saw the three Japs fall as he swept by onto the field. He ruddered the Zero around the long way, and sent it streaking down the runway. Then he pulled back slightly on the stick, and the Zero was clear and prop-clawing up into the sky.

"You're still my sweetheart, Lady Luck!" were

the first crazy words to come off his lips. "You sure are!"

Nosing over off the climb, he circled around to the left and stared down. Coming up out of the very center of the oblong of green was Jimmy Joyce in the pit of the other Zero. Red waggled his wings crazily and waved his free hand over his head.

But there was no time for greetings now. Half-way along the left side of the air strip a Zero shot out into the open, whirled around the long way and started to take off.

"That's what you think, Jap rat!" Randall howled, and stuck the nose of his Zero almost straight down.

An instant later holes appeared in his left wing, and a section of glass in his opened hatch flew away. Ground gunners were banging away at him to drive him off so that a Jap-manned Zero could get into the air. Red ripped straight down on the Zero and gave it all his guns. The plane acted as though it had caught its undercarriage on an invisible wire stretched across the air strip. Its prop cut into the ground and threw earth in all directions. It whipped up onto its nose, fell over on its back, and then blew up in a fountain of flaming embers.

Red did not see the Zero explode. He was just pulling out of his dive when he caught sight of a Mitsubishi MK-11 swerving out onto the field in a headlong take-off. Its wheels were just clearing the air strip when Randall got within gun range. In spite of Red's fire, the Jap managed to reach an altitude of about fifty feet. That proved to be his ceiling, however. His Mitsubishi came apart at the seams, burst into flame and slithered earthward.

By then Randall had reached the far end of the field. He zoomed to curve around, but changed his mind when he spotted a group of fifty Jap soldiers in open ranks charging across the air strip toward some of Wilkins' raiders storming a building. One look at the situation and he dropped his Zero down like a comet. He fired his guns and pumped rudder to wag the nose back and forth and increase his fire area. Ten of the Japs stopped running. They fell on their faces and lay still. The others almost reached their objective before Randall could catch them in his sights. Those who did not die from his guns died as Wilkins' men, now conscious of the danger behind them, whirled around.

Randall zoomed to avoid slamming straight into the jungle trees that bordered that side of the strip. As he climbed, he turned his head to look back on the field. At the far end of the strip a Jap Zero was prop-clawing up into the air. For a brief instant he thought it was Jimmy Joyce zooming up from ground strafing, but then he noticed that the markings on the climbing Zero were not those he had seen on Jimmy's plane.

"One getting away!" he bellowed and kicked his Zero around in the dime turn that only a Zero can make. "One getting away, and I can't reach him. Jimmy! Where are you, Jimmy!"

As though his flying pal had heard him, Jimmy shot out from under the jungle trees on the other side of the air strip and drilled straight up toward the escaping Jap. The guns of Joyce's Zero stabbed out jets of flame and the tracer smoke made lines in the air straight up to the Jap's plane. It staggered over to one side, dropped sharply by the nose, and enjoyed the questionable distinction over the other fallen Jap planes of hitting the ground before it actually exploded and burst into flame. To add insult to injury, Jimmy wheeled over out of his zoom and drilled a group of half a dozen Japs who tried to sneak across one corner of the landing strip in the smoke of the explosion.

"Pretty as a picture!" Randall shouted. And then as he caught sight of another bunch of Japs trying to do the same thing at his end of the air strip, he added quickly, "Just like this, hey, kiddo?"

Moments later he and Jimmy whipped their

Zeros up and down the length of the air strip, eyes skinned for any Jap planes taking off, or groups of Japs on the ground giving Wilkins' men trouble.

But they saw no signs of either. The smoke from burning planes grew less and less, though it hung over everything like a dirty white shroud. Neither saw spurts of flame from rifles or machine guns, nor the sharp, clear-cut flashes of exploding hand grenades. After a while they saw some of Wilkins' raiders come running out into the open, waving their guns.

If Randall needed any further sign that the "party" was over for him as far as flying was concerned, the Nakajima radial in the nose of his Zero did not. It began to cough and sputter. At first he thought a fuel line had weakened, but when he looked at his watch he saw the true reason . . . and was dumbfounded. He had been aloft for an hour and a half, which was the time limit for Zeros of the type he and Jimmy were flying.

"An hour and a half?" he gasped, and peered

at the second hand to make sure it was moving. "Why, it seems I've been in the air only five minutes. How things happen, and you don't feel anything!"

The last came off his lips as he saw that his left sleeve was red with blood. He gaped at it in disbelief, for when he moved the arm he felt no pain. He reached over with his right hand and quickly pulled up the sleeve. A bullet crease ran diagonally across his forearm, but there was absolutely no sensation of pain.

"Maybe I'm just one tough guy who can take it," he said with a grin as he quickly grabbed the controls again.

When he had set the Zero down on the air strip, he twisted around in his seat to see Jimmy land about twenty yards away from him.

By the time they had legged out, a bunch of "Wild Willie" Wilkins' raiders were out there to greet them, and shouting praise that made them blush with modesty and pleasure too. Kagi was there, eyes popping with pride, and a smile that stretched from ear to ear.

Major Wilkins appeared out of nowhere. "Never saw a show like it!" he cried, shaking hands with each of them. "Everything went off like clockwork. You gave us what we needed to really pull it over. Without you two up there, I wouldn't dare say what might have happened."

"It's *all* over?" Randall asked, still unable to grasp the fact that complete victory had been attained. "You mean . . . ?"

He stumbled over his words and waved his hand toward either side of the air strip where isolated clouds of smoke were still lifting up to blend in with the overcast. Major Wilkins grinned through his whiskers and nodded.

"Clean as a whistle," he said. "Caught them fair offguard. A few got away in the jungle, but we don't need to worry about them. We got a fine loot, too. It'll last us for many a day."

"What do you plan to do next, sir?" Jimmy

Joyce asked. "The Japs are bound to hear of this, and send bombers over in force. They might even send troops to retake the field if they can."

"Let them come with their blasted bombers or troops!" "Wild Willie" Wilkins said with a laugh. "We won't be here by then. The place is of no use to us. If the Nip wants what we leave of his planes and stores, he's welcome to them. I've a fancy, though, he'll drop the whole thing, even the strip itself when he sees what we've done to it. We'll be on our way to another little project I have in mind by the time the Nip gets here. We'll be off to give the Japs at Buna something to worry about. I only wish that you two were coming along."

"What was that?" Red blurted out in surprise. "Joyce and I can't . . . ?"

"Afraid not," Major Wilkins said with a sad smile. "You're removed from my command, now that this business is over. Major Pratt's orders. He wants you back at Seven Mile, where he needs you."

"But how . . . ?" Red began.

"Been in radio contact with him, of course," Wilkins explained. "The radio hut was the first thing we went after. Couldn't afford to give the Japs time to use or destroy it. We cleaned them out fast, and took over. Told Major Pratt about you two, and he asked if there was fuel to take you two there. I told him there was. He asked that I send you along just as soon as I could spare you."

"You mean, it's worse at Port Moresby, sir?" Jimmy asked in a worried voice.

"On the contrary, much better than it was when you left," Major Wilkins replied. "Pratt told me that the Milne Bay bombing turned out fine. Not as many Japs as they had expected, and they made it too hot for those there to stay. We took some air losses, though, and Major Pratt wants you two at Seven Mile to help out in case the Nip starts anything new. With this base smashed, I have a feeling he'll take some time out to plot a different plan to get Moresby."

"And that plan will go up in smoke, too!" Randall said grimly. Then with a little sad smile, he added, "Back to Moresby, eh? Well, it's been a swell vacation, if you can call it that. But, wait a minute, sir! The boys at Seven Mile and there-abouts have itchy fingers. They may let fly at us as we come sailing in in these Zeros."

"You don't need to worry about that," Major Wilkins said. "You're to time your flight to arrive there at seventeen hours. Major Pratt is spreading the word that you'll arrive then, and issuing orders not to shoot. By the way, the Major sent his heartiest congratulations to you both. No end pleased with the job you pulled off for me. He said that when you arrived at Seven Mile he was going to make war history."

"War history, sir?" Red echoed with a puzzled frown.

"Yes," "Wild Willie" Wilkins said with a chuckle. "He says he's going to be the first Ameri-can squadron commander in this war to run out onto his own field and shake hands with a couple of Zero pilots!"

—THE END—

RED RANDALL IN THE ALEUTIANS

AT THAT very instant, as though the hands of invisible giants had pulled it aside, the world of fog through which the Catalina PBY had been plowing split apart to reveal a vast expanse of slate-gray water ahead and below the flying boat. The area of clear air extended straight up toward the heavens, and fog, sea, sky, and the PBY were bathed in the weird pale light of the Arctic sun. It was like flying into a mysterious fairyland, and for an instant neither Red Randall nor Jimmy Joyce could utter a sound. And then they looked at each other and spoke almost in the same breath.

"Look! Dead ahead! A baby flat-top and two destroyers. And they're Jap!"

Several miles ahead and just sliding out of sight into a curtain of fog was a Nipponese baby aircraft carrier with an escort of two destroyers. They were gone in a moment, leaving behind three long lines of milky wake.

"Japs!" Randall gasped. "A carrier task force. Didn't I tell you, Jimmy, that . . . ?"

The chilling note of the alarm buzzer cut off the rest of his words. Immediately followed the excited voice of Aviation Machinist Mate Pat Hall from the rear gun turret.

"Enemy aircraft coming down at six o'clock! They look like Zeros to me. Boy! Look at those babies travel! They . . . !"

That was all the others aboard the flying boat heard of Pat Hall's voice over the intercom. The air all about suddenly shook and trembled with the savage yammer of aerial machine-gun fire. And streams of orange red tracers slashed down past the nose of the Catalina.

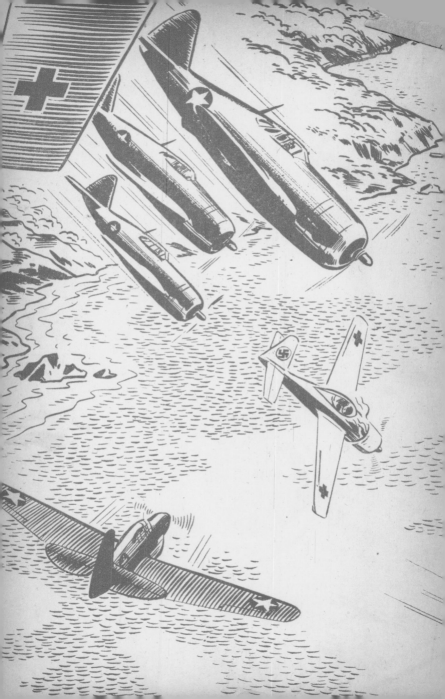